MW01247900

DEATH ON MOSHUP'S ROCK

Z Z RAWLINS

Death on Moshup's Rock
Copyright © 2023 by Z. Z. Rawlins, Noir House, LLC.

This is a work of fiction. Names, characters, businesses, places, events, locales, and incidents are either the products of the author's imagination or used in a fictitious manner.

All rights reserved. No part of this publication may be reproduced, distributed, or transmitted in any form or by any means, including photocopying, recording, or other electronic or mechanical methods, without the prior written permission of the publisher, except in the case of brief quotations embodied in critical reviews and certain other noncommercial uses permitted by copyright law. Please do not participate in or encourage piracy of copyrighted materials in violation of the author's rights.

Editing by The Pro Book Editor
Interior and Cover Design by IAPS.rocks
Photography by Linda Zarro

eBook ISBN: 979-8-9886203-0-3
Audiobook ISBN: 979-8-9886203-1-0
Paperback ISBN: 979-8-9886203-2-7
Hardcover ISBN: 979-8-9886203-3-4

      1. Main category—Fiction / Mystery & Detective
      2. Other category—Fiction / Thrillers / Crime

First Edition

Dedicated to my father, who is a
bigger man than he knows.

TABLE OF CONTENTS

Chapter 1: The Homecoming 1

Chapter 2: The Chief 17

Chapter 3: Death and Diamonds 29

Chapter 4: Fishing Is a Living, Sometimes 49

Chapter 5: The Cat's Tongue 61

Chapter 6: Hail Mary 67

Chapter 7: I Love Funerals 77

Chapter 8: People Are Not That Complicated 87

Chapter 9: Fires 93

Chapter 10: The Finger 111

Chapter 11: The Drugs 123

Chapter 12: The Woods 135

Chapter 13: The Triangle 143

Chapter 14: Everything Perfect is Full of Flaws 155

Backstory: The Court Cases 183

About the Author 185

Acknowledgments 187

CHAPTER 1
THE HOMECOMING

T HE *ISLANDER* PULLED INTO VINEYARD Haven harbor at 8:45 p.m. With a few bumps against the huge wood pylons, she straightened herself with a back-and-forth of the motors before the gangway lowered, fastened to the ferry, and the Steamship Authority night crew hollered all clear. The metal port doors of the ferry swung heavily and latched. Parents dragging exhausted kids, college students in sweatpants, and Sunday-night turnover renters from the mainland filed down the plank quietly, too tired to break the evening's silence.

Except Ray Cillo. He came tripping down the gang-plank with an over-the-top guffaw, his arms around two girls in tiny shorts and USA T-shirts. The girls stumbled over their suitcases; some joke about Irish Setters Ray told ten minutes ago snowballed into hyperventilating hysterics. Ray had spotted them forty-five minutes ear-lier, boarding in Woods Hole, keyed in on their Scot-Brit-Irish-foreign accents, and extended a gentlemanly arm to the ship's bar for rounds of Sutter Home mini bottles.

"We cruising, we boozing," said Ray. The redheads had giggled, the overture accepted, and the rest of the ferry ride became a captive stage for the yarn of Ray's life—only child of struggling immigrants, Air Force pilot shot down in Iraq, decorated Boston homicide detective, torch-bearer for a cold-hearted woman he couldn't stop loving—told with the tenderness and grit of an Emily Brontë novel. The girls sopped it up. They were coming to work a job scooping ice cream. The Vineyard looked like a fun place to spend the summer. Little had they expected the dynamic and entrancing Ray to welcome them to America and offer so much advice on life.

The trio reached the bottom of the gangway, Ray gave them both a squeeze. Giggling, the girls extricated Ray's long arms and said to come by the ice cream place. He threw up his hands and asked where they were going, but they walked on, waving kisses goodbye. Ray smirked, thinking of another joke about American-style hospitality when a car horn started blaring.

"Jesus Christ."

At the end of the pier, a white Volvo idled with Ray's mother, Anne, behind the wheel. She leaned her fist into the horn again and waved furiously to get in the car. Ray let out a long sigh, opened the car door, and threw his bags in the back seat. It was a nice ferry ride, at least.

"Who were those women? Do you know them?" Anne snipped.

"No, I just met them on the way over. You look gorgeous as always, Ma."

Anne shook her head, screwed up her red lips. She had on a leopard-print raincoat from Bamberger's, circa 1980, her red hair bunned up under a turban. Diamond earrings, Foster Grant wraparounds, heavy perfume. The car jerked as she mashed the pedal, pursing her lips to hold back all the things her son had done wrong since he was too young to remember, or at least since the last time she had seen him.

"What? I've not even been on this island for five minutes and you're already upset. What did I do now?"

"You know, Ray, when are you gonna grow up? I keep waiting but it's not happening."

"What are you talking about? I met some decently dressed, attractive women with no visible diseases and ensured their native voyage to Martha's Vineyard was as enjoyable as it could be. You know, if we all treated foreigners as nicely as I treated them, we would have fewer world wars. That's a fact."

"Oh yeah?" Anne shook her head and smiled. Ray could bullshit like no other.

"You see, girls like that, they're looking for someone with experience…"

"Oh, you got that, Ray."

"So I'm doing my civic duty as an American, and as a frequent visitor to the island, to provide them my very experienced perspective. How are you going to argue with that?" Ray's face started to crack as the bullshit got deeper.

"What ever happened to that nice blonde girl you were dating? Her family had money."

"You know what the secret is for rich women? They expect you to buy everything. Hand to God I never was so broke to keep one person happy. I was on my way to living in a cardboard box on the street. Nah, I'm back to dating cheap women with low expectations. And

tank you were alone. No one asked you questions. No one
passed judgment with just a look. In jail, there was no
booze, no women, and no internet, but there was also no
mother. Ray laughed to himself.

"Ray, you're here to get yourself together, right?
You're supposed to be taking it easy and, you know, fig-
uring out how to get your job back."

"Yeah, yeah. I will. It's just for a while."

Anne went quiet. They drove down Main Street in
Tisbury toward West Chop. The streetlights stopped about
a mile out of town. After that, it was a dark road and a life

without vices. Whatever joke Ray had told the redheads on the ferry, he couldn't remember it now.

You dumbass, he thought. *You had it all figured out.* The political hopscotch through the police department had seemed like an easy game. Kiss the right ass, bend the rules when no one was watching, fake up a few confessions, and who cared? All in the line of duty. To protect and serve. So what if he broke a guy's wrist to get a confession once? Deadbeat loser bound for life in prison dealing oxy by an elementary school deserved it. Ray's partner in the room had said nothing, and then brought it up to save his own ass when the department crusaded for a kinder and gentler police force. Ray was in the crosshairs, a tough white guy with a big chip and a big mouth. Ray was told to take leave. To let the political winds blow.

That was June. After thoroughly stinking up his apartment, Ray put his minimal possessions and some beach clothes in a suitcase and decided to hide out on the island. His gut said he was tired. His ego said he was lonely, irritated, and in no mood to talk to anyone.

His mother turned the car off Main Street onto Juniper Lane, more of a long driveway with two other houses than a real road. In the dark, a porch light shone on the winterized two-story bungalow she and Ray's father, Carl, bought back in the 1970s when island real estate was affordable and middle-class families from Boston bought summer places. It looked the same as it did in the 1970s, with some window dressing and new shingles that dated it to Hurricane Andrew. Before he died, Carl added a room above the garage so he could watch the Weather Channel and drink in private. Ray looked up at the window to his dad's old hideout and claimed it as his own now.

It didn't take long to unpack, plug in his devices, pull out the couch. It was a million years old, thin and flat as an army cot. It creaked under his weight, the only noise in the otherwise silent, dark room. Ray laid his head on a pillow, flat as a padded envelope, and closed his eyes, doing something he thought was breathing exercises to stop his racing mind.

There was no city din out the window. No women, no police work. Just conversations in his head he couldn't stop, the endless replay of how he got it so wrong, how he was set up after years of getting the crap beat out of him for little more than a teacher's salary plus pension. He twisted on his side to reach for his phone, and a pain shot through his back, an old injury from falling off a wall into a fence. He reached farther for the painkillers in his travel bag. At thirty-six he was starting to groan in the morning, get caffeine headaches, walk with a heavy shuffle. His thick, wavy hair was salt and pepper like his father's, but too soon. He'd hoped his father would appreciate what it took to be a cop. His mother definitely had. She was a prize-fighter herself. Tough old bag.

Ray went to the kitchen to get a drink. Anne looked up at him with her iced tea.

"My back is bothering me again. I gotta go to the doctor tomorrow. I need you to drive me."

"Where's the doctor?"

"Five corners, not that far. I gotta be there ten o'clock. And if you want me to, I'll call up Comcast tomorrow about the internet. Maybe they can get someone out here, but it's the holiday."

"I'd appreciate it."

Anne sat across from him. The ice tinkled in her glass. She glowed under the kitchen light and stared at him for a long minute.

"What happened, Ray? I thought you were doing okay. When'd you fall off the wagon?"

Ray looked at her glass. His thoughts were noisy and empty. There was no clean way to explain anything.

"It's been a lot of things, Ma. I came out of the academy with big ideas, didn't I?" He laughed. "I thought I was going to, you know, make the world right. The world seems against me. I think I'm depressed."

"Don't you give me that psychology mumbo-jumbo. Are you starving? Are you out digging ditches? No! Your grandparents lived through a real depression—the Great Depression. Don't talk to me about being depressed. You got it so good you don't know the first th—"

"All right, all right. So I'm not depressed. I just screwed up, okay?"

Anne leaned in. Her eyes were steady. "Look, you're not going to make anything right if you can't keep it together. You gotta figure out what's gonna make you stick to one thing and be successful. If you're gonna stay in this police business, you gotta get in line. You know, you're just like your father. Wouldn't listen to anyone. Couldn't work for anyone. Used to think he was the smartest guy ever. Well, we know that story." She laughed.

Ray couldn't hold back a grin. "All those crazy ideas. Remember when he went to business importing fancy Italian kids' shoes with pointy toes? Or the no-questions-asked pawn shop that also sold fake dog poop?"

"You know, your father, he was just trying to make it. We had nothing for a long time, and having nothing, well, it changes you. We didn't want you to ever go without." Anne looked absently at an enormous three-diamond cocktail ring on her finger, letting it sparkle in the kitchen light. Carl brought it home to her one day as a surprise birthday gift.

She got up from the table. "Go to bed, Ray. We need to leave here by nine-thirty. Get some rest."

The next day was overcast, windy, humid. Ray and Anne pulled up to her doctor's office, an unassuming, gray-shingled building in a row of other gray-shingled, unassuming buildings. Dr. Dennis Spahr's small waiting room didn't offer much to wait with: a few maps of the Cape and Islands, outdated magazines. The young woman behind the reception deck was young, dark hair, very attractive. Ray wondered about the inventive ways she'd learned to say "no."

"Mrs. Cillo! Good to see you."

Dr. Spahr was thin and blond, with a sharp nose and chin that made Ray think of a chirping canary. The doc held out a hand and helped Anne out of her chair.

"Oh, Doc, how are you? My back is killing me."

"Same trouble? Let's get you in and have a look-see, Mrs. Cillo. Rachel, can you pull Mrs. Cillo's file, please?"

"How's your family?" Anne asked. "Are they coming for the weekend? My son is staying with me right now."

"How nice you remembered! My brother and his kids are coming over on the ferry this afternoon." Dr. Spahr swept the file off the desk in one hand and made an escorting motion into the examination room with the other.

Spahr. A brother. He knew a Charles Spahr from the academy. Smart, cocky guy. Ray's mind went digging up fragments of the past, like a dog digging for bones buried years ago. He chewed his lower lip while his mother ambled into the exam room, then walked to the reception desk.

"Hey. Excuse me."

Rachel looked up with intense green eyes. She was striking, almost intimidating to look at.

"Hmm?"

"Does Dr. Spahr have a brother by chance? Charles Spahr?"

"I honestly wouldn't know." Green Eyes looked away. "I don't know anything about his family." She turned back to the computer on her desk as quick as swatting a fly.

"Thanks."

Ray muttered to himself and turned toward the window. He picked up an outdated magazine with a picture of the governor at South Beach and tried to stop digging for information. This hole had no bone in it, but it had a pretty girl.

Anne came out of the examination room thirty minutes later, leaning on Dr. Spahr's arm, and with a new prescription for painkillers. She looked up into his face as if she'd just been on a wonderful date and couldn't wait to be asked out again.

"Thank you, Dr. Spahr. You know what I need. Not like the other doctors that won't even give you an aspirin."

"Anytime, Mrs. Cillo. Let me know how that works out for you. Rachel, remind me to follow up with Mrs. Cillo in a few weeks to check how the prescription is going."

Anne smiled right past her son. "All right, let's go. We gotta stop at the Stop and Shop on the way back."

———

Ray spent the rest of the morning and early afternoon driving his mother around for errands and things she suddenly needed now that she had a chauffeur. He didn't mind too much, even in what she called "island summer traffic," which was nothing compared to the jammed highways of the mainland.

He rolled the windows down and took Beach Road, a pencil of asphalt with a beach on one side and a lagoon on the other. It was an undeniably gorgeous day, as gorgeous as Rachel's green eyes. The blue-and-white sky, the foaming waves, some girls in bathing suits biking down the road soothed Ray. He eased off the gas pedal and relaxed.

At the Stop and Shop, Ray picked up the two island papers, the *Gazette* and the *Times*. Top of the fold on the *Times* were some kids at a farm. He tucked it under his arm. Top of the fold on the *Gazette*: tall ship, USS *Alabama*, ready for another season. He flipped to the middle of the paper: restaurant menus and real estate. Back of the paper: want ads. Curious, he skimmed and spotted "Part-time security guards needed. Must clear background check, drug test. Inquire at Tisbury police station." Ray folded the paper, shoved it in the shopping bag with the frozen chicken. It sounded like a cake walk, if he needed something to do. Summer rent-a-cops spent more time watching people than apprehending them.

On the drive home, the idea grew. Why not give himself something to do? It wouldn't interfere with his time off, as it wasn't real police duty—it was private contract work. What could it pay? Twenty-five dollars an hour? Why not just see what would happen? And it might play nicely with the people he had to play nice with. He would give his boss a ring and chat it over.

Bright and chipper, and eager to share his brainchild of an idea early the next morning, Ray rang police captain Peter Boyer. Boyer sounded confused. And why not, it was 8:27 a.m..

"Raymond Cillo," said Peter, slowly enunciating between slurps of coffee, "surprised to hear from you. I hope you're someplace where they put a pink umbrella in your drink."

Ray snorted. "Not quite. I'm on the Vineyard—my mom has a place. I was going stir crazy so I came over to the rock. No little umbrellas yet. But hey, I want to run something by you."

"I'm all ears."

"Are there any rules, guidelines, you know, about working as a private security guard in Dukes County while I'm on voluntary leave?"

Peter paused for so long that Ray started listening for breathing.

"If it's a private company, I'm pretty sure there are no rules against it."

More silence.

"Ray, the point of time off is to take time off. You need to come back here with demonstrated progress that you have a fresh perspective. Voluntary time off rather than mandatory leave means it's up to you to show the department you've made adjustments. I'm leaving it up to you to show that level of responsibility. You need to do what you think is best for your career."

Ray liked his captain, but this kind of department-speak lit his hair on fire. Process and procedure was all that mattered. "I understand. I'll check out this private company and let you know. Thanks for your support, Peter."

Grinning, he ended the call. Then he asked his mother to borrow the car.

———

The small Tisbury police station was empty when he arrived. There was nowhere to sit, so he leaned his elbows on the counter. In a room to the right, he saw a few guys in blue cargo pants and Tisbury Police T-shirts. They weren't doing any work that day, just catching up on their foot dangling.

"Hello!"

One of the men slowly walked to the counter. He didn't seem too friendly, too eager, or too interested in Ray.

"How can I help?"

"Hi, I'm here about the part-time security job."

"Oh. Sure. I'm Officer Sawyer."

He held out his hand, but the dulled expression didn't change. "I need you to fill out these forms, and I need to see your IDs."

Sawyer handed Ray four sheets of pink-and-white forms in six-point font, requesting his consent for background checks and drug tests for Security Extension Services. Nowhere did they mention the hours or rate.

"What exactly is the job, and what's it pay?"

"It's twenty to thirty hours a week through Labor Day. We have all kinds of assignments but mostly patrol."

"Will I be working for a private company or the town?"

"It's just like it says at the top." Sawyer seemed suddenly agitated. He pointed to the name on the form. "This is for SES. You're gonna work for them but as part of town police. Tisbury police. So, a uniform that looks like the one I have on, but it'll say SES. To get paid, you gotta go online. They don't pay me, so I don't know how it works."

Sawyer's attitude was winning all kinds of points with Ray. He pulled the forms slowly off the counter, glaring.

"How about a pen? Can I get one of those?"

Ray spent the next twenty minutes painfully printing information into little boxes. By the time he finished, his hand had a cramp.

"How long will the review process take?"

"I don't know. SES will call you."

———————————

Ray waited. While he waited, July fourth came and the island made its annual crescendo: splashed up some fireworks, fried a few thousand clams, and the Vineyard Haven band played "Stars and Stripes Forever" in the town gazebo.

Ray heard the dull roar of the holiday from his mother's porch. Half of him missed whatever action there was to be found, the other half was too busy nursing a bruised ego and waiting for a phone call like a desperate teenager. He had no friends, not even a dog to walk. One day, he'd driven to the gas station to fill the tank, just to have a reason to move from his Adirondack chair.

Anne was enjoying the company and the help. They sat and read the twice-weekly papers, talked about people on the island, and did what they wanted. Ray played the helpful son, tightening up loose door hinges and fixing the ancient garage-door opener. Anne cooked her signature clam chowder with corn bread. It was relaxing, comforting. His mother's painkillers seemed to be working—she was in a chatty mood most of the time, telling stories of Ray's father, Carl, and their early days running different businesses, including a jewelry store, a furniture store, a pizzeria, a barber shop.

"That's when his favorite phrase was 'money is not the issue.' so I knew we were doing well," she'd say. "Otherwise, money is the only issue."

Ray could feel his mother had claimed her stake here. After his father died, she lost many of her old friends, the wives of other men Carl knew. Coming to the island, she found a new social circle and figured out how the grapevine worked. Checkout lines were ground zero as Ray had found out at the Stop and Shop the week before. Over bananas and swordfish, islanders gossiped about who'd filed for divorce, who'd died, who was closing after a bad season, the house listed for a million plus with a sump pump problem.

———————————•••——————————

Monday after the fourth, SES called. The news came back mostly good, with some follow-up requests to his department. SES talked to Boyer, who gave a cautious thumbs up. By tomorrow, the company would make its decision.

Ray told his mother about the tentative offer while they finished up the chowder that night. She was not impressed with his judgment.

"You're gonna work security? Why can't you work in a shop or something? Do something where you're not dealing with crazy people or idiots on vacation. I know you—you're supposed to be taking it easy, getting yourself together. Your boss says this is okay?" Her eyes flashed with disappointment.

"I saw the ad and thought it was a good thing for me. You know, get to know the people around here." Ray skated along on his thin logic. He lowered his voice. "Look, Ma, I know you're concerned, but if it's not working for the town, then the department can't legally stop me. I took time off voluntarily, or at least, that's what my record is gonna show. Besides, I called Boyer, and he approved it. So I checked the boxes. I followed the process."

"I can feel it in my bones. This is a bad idea." Anne sucked her teeth, leaned back in her chair, and brought one knee up under her arm, her pose of pontification.

Ray refused to be a teenager again, living under her rules.

"This is light stuff. Traffic duty. Lets me ease into dealing with people and confrontation. Life is a journey, Ma, and I have to keep going." Ray was borderline convincing himself. "Besides, it's the island. You know nothing is gonna happen."

CHAPTER 2
THE CHIEF

"I NEED EVERYONE TO CALM DOWN." Mathias Winnetukqet stood at the front of the Gay Head Community Center and banged his fist into the podium.

The building was hot, packed with Wampanoag tribe members and townspeople in full pandemonium. Mathias, over six feet and plenty wide, had beads of sweat running from the dark hair he wore in braids, a tip to his Native American heritage. He was shouting at the crowd and getting nowhere.

At the back of the community center was a kid's party karaoke machine. He ripped the chord out of the wall, slammed it on the podium and plugged it in again, hoping whatever came out of it—his voice in autotune or pop music—would get the crowd's attention. He switched it on, cranked the volume all the way.

"Hey! I need everyone to quiet down immediately. Please sit down."

The tiny, over-driven amplifier squealed, and the room's noise level ticked down a few decibels. It was the first of many meetings for the town's residents and the Massachusetts Wampanoag tribe to hear plans for making the community center into a Class II gaming facility. The non-Wampanoag residents of the town, and some Wampanoags too, had an over-my-dead-body attitude, mortified that the crass and commercial enterprise of gambling could even be considered on Martha's Vineyard. Mathias and his supporters had been building up to the meeting for months, touting the benefits of gaming revenue as the silver bullet to quell a spike in drug use, unemployment, and kick-start a "cultural rebuilding program."

"I know everyone here is fired up about this issue. I'm going to read through the proposal. While I do, I need everyone to be quiet until the end. Then we'll get to questions. If anyone tries to stop this meeting from happening, you will be arrested, and I'm not kidding. There are police outside."

The room was as tense and angry as it was hot, but it was finally still. With a slow hand, Mathias pulled his glasses out of his shirt pocket, spread a crinkled paper on the podium, and read the proposal into the tiny microphone.

"The Wampanoag Tribe of Gay Head, under the rights given it under the 1988 Indian Gaming Regulatory Act, the IRGA for short, in the state of Massachusetts, hereby intends to establish a Class II gaming facility using tribal funds, to be run by tribe members, for the benefits of tribe members, on tribal lands of Gay Head. The Wampanoag Tribe of Gay Head is openly and legally exercising its right under the IRGA similar to the exercise of these rights by the Wampanoag tribe of Mashpee, Massachusetts, when establishing a similar gaming facility on their tribal lands. Wampanoag tribal leadership from both Gay Head and off-island held a vote on May sixteenth of this year with a ten-seven decision in favor of the conversion to a gaming facility, with seven abstaining."

Mathias looked over his glasses at the crowd sprawled on folding chairs, leaning against walls, some sitting on the floor. No electrical. No AC. Some fanned themselves with copies of the proposal that had been handed out at the door, but otherwise, not a feather could move in the stuffed room. All eyes were on Mathias. Eyes of anger, disgust, sympathy, admiration.

Mathias continued, "As the elected tribal leader, it is my privilege to carry out the will of the tribal people and see their intent carried throu—"

"That's a load of crap, Winnetukqet." Daniel Vanderhoop, a dissenting Wampanoag, released venom from the front row. "That vote was mostly off-islanders, and you know it. You're selling this town off for a few dollars, and you don't care."

"I'm sorry you feel that way, Daniel. This vote was done in accordance with all bylaws and procedures. You can check the records yourself and see who voted for—"

"If it was left up to the islanders, this would not be happening," Daniel interrupted, unfazed. "Let the people who live here decide if they want a cheap bingo hall. The answer will be no." He gestured to the room at large. Scattered cheers.

"Let the islanders decide!" hurled from the back.

"Winnetukqet is a traitor to his tribe," whipped another.

"A vote is a vote. Get over it and move on," braved a third.

"Let them build it. We'll burn it to the ground."

The crowd was raucous again. Mathias felt his fury building a second time when suddenly a strange hush came over the place, like all the oxygen was sucked out of the room. Heads turned to the front of the center. Andrew Cogswell, the town building inspector and arguably the most powerful person in Gay Head, darkened the double-door entrance. He folded tan, hairless arms across his chest, a tear in his "Salty Johnson's Clam Bar" T-shirt glimpsed a Tazmanian Devil tattoo on his peck. With a John-Wayne worthy swagger, he walked slowly through the middle of the room to the podium. Mathias's face tightened, his eyes narrowed. He put a hand over the microphone.

"What's this, Drew?" Mathias, a good head taller, stared him down.

Andrew's smirk didn't melt. He took a folded paper from his cargo pants and announced, "I'm issuing you an immediate cease and desist order. As your one and only town building inspector, I'm telling you no land or buildings can be used for gaming purposes under town law."

Mathias breathed in and out like a bull, squeezing the tiny mic with his huge fist.

Drew continued, "You can't do anything because you gotta get a permit, and I'm not gonna give it to you. If you try to build anything here, I'll rip it down when your guys leave for the day." An uproar of cheers and clapping broke out as the paper flitted off the podium. "Too bad, Chief."

"The IRGA supersedes town laws. That's from the Fed," Mathias shot back in a forced whisper. Then he pulled himself away and uncovered the microphone to address the raucous room.

"I'd like to thank Mr. Cogswell for stopping by. He seems to think he has jurisdiction to shut this project down, but he's wrong. The meeting is going to continue as planned. Please take your seats so we can continue."

"Oh, you can have your meeting, but this town will never have a casino as long as I'm alive."

Andrew, grenade lobbed and exploded, didn't bother to look back as Mathias watched him get into his idling pickup, wink at the police officers in the parking lot, and then burn down the gravel road.

When Drew was out of sight, Mathias waved eagerly for two of the officers to come inside. In a minute the community center was as still and tense as it was before. Exasperated cries of, "Come on," and, "Is this really necessary?" floated up in the room.

"Many of you know Officer Stevens, Officer Dodd. I called them up here not to strong-arm anyone, but to make it clear if anyone disrupts this meeting again, they will be escorted out of here." Mathias cracked a smile and added, "By one of the island's finest."

No one laughed.

In the dirt parking lot, Officer Jerry DeBettencourt was on his phone with the Edgartown police chief.

"Hi, Tom, what's up?"

"Hey, Jerry, I need you to send some of your men down to the airport."

"What for?"

"We need cruisers as escorts for the governor's party. He's landing in an hour. He's bringing his family and staffers and yadda yadda. Twenty people in all, I think. We had a time on the plane but didn't find out until just now that he was bringing an entourage."

"The governor isn't using his own detail?"

"His chief of staff called here and asked us to send whatever we had. They need more than what they already brought over on the ferry."

Jerry looked at the cruisers in the parking lot and sized up who could go. Ray was in one of the cruisers, looking bored.

"We're at the tribe meeting now. I can leave a few here and come down there myself with a part-timer and a few cruisers. That's should do ya."

"Thank you kindly." The chief hung up.

Jerry walked to Ray and smiled. "You're the big-city guy, right? I've got another assignment for you."

———————

Governor Phil McKenna, neatly pressed in Nantucket red shorts with tiny, embroidered sailboats, white loafers, and a frock of blond hair, grabbed his pretty wife's hand and stepped from his Gulfstream G550 onto the tarmac. Together, they waved to the press from *The Boston Globe*, *Martha's Vineyard Times*, and the *Gazette* newspapers, waving with the enthusiasm of a first-term administration six points behind in his reelection race. He'd been trailing his opponent for three weeks, so to pick up some traction, he'd directed his staff to start Operation Photo Blitz: pictures with the archbishop of Boston, pictures marching in rallies, pictures playing basketball with the underprivileged, pictures shopping on "tax-free sales day." The strategy seemed to be working, as his gap closed from eight points to six. Walking across the tarmac, followed by two handsome and shaggy-haired sons, McKenna held up his wife's hand while they waved, making their signature move, a human *W*. Reporters had a field day interpreting what the hell that meant.

Next out of the plane came his chief of staff, campaign manager, press secretary, personal doctor, private security, and some people paid to be busy. About two dozen people stood behind the airport fence, watching the big to-do. They looked on with polite but blank faces, as they would look upon a duck that landed on their front lawn. The governor and his family waved and smiled to everyone, loaded into polished black Suburbans with official-looking seals. It was a very small airport, and the size of the governor's entourage cracked the island's unpretentiousness like an elephant stepping on a peanut.

Ray watched the scene, as curious as anyone else. He hadn't met many politicians and never one this high up. Governor McKenna looked like any other rich vacationer except surrounded by a payroll of public servants. Ray's job was to drive the cruiser behind the governor's SUV to Farm Neck Golf Club, where a flock of people were waiting to shake hands and take pictures. The other officers were to escort the remaining vehicles to the governor's house in Chilmark, where they would set up vacation HQ.

It was a dull assignment. The hardest part for Ray would be keeping his mouth shut and his eyes open.

The cars turned off Airport Road to County Road, then took a right onto a discreet wooded driveway. At the front of the drive, two antique wagon wheels between manicured wildflowers held up a wood sign for "Farm Neck Golf Club members only." If you weren't reminded to pay your fifteen thousand dollar annual dues, you might drive right past the place and never know it was there.

The drive to the club house was long and winding and made of crushed stone. On either side, golf carts floated over emerald grasses. It was an oasis in an oasis for the out-of-sight rich. The clubhouse was a sprawling three-story, gray-shingled mansion, crisply trimmed in white, with a long stone veranda and French doors meeting the trim cut edges of putting greens. Rows of hydrangeas in full bloom, arborvitaes cut in tight cones surrounded a parking lot of luxury cars. Lots of white people in pastel pants stood at the end of the driveway and clapped quietly when the governor and his family got out.

"At least they have a sense of humor," Ray muttered to himself.

Jerry addressed his guys. "This place has been checked out already, so we need to just keep our eyes and ears open, watch the crowd for anything unusual. If the governor splits off from his family, I'll follow him. You guys watch Mrs. McKenna and the sons."

It was a scorcher. The humidity hung like sandbags and seemed to slow time. He cursed the chump twenty-five dollars per hour before taxes as unjustified for this torture.

The governor didn't seem to notice the heat at all. Neither did the golfers. Ray saw McKenna make his way down the line, shaking hands, patting shoulders, saying first names, posing for pictures. A few asked McKenna about his golf game, what kind of clubs he used, and if he could join for a round.

Ray meandered his way to the shade of a tree, took a glug of water. From nowhere, the governor's wife appeared. She reached out with a desperate face and fell into his arms.

"Mrs. McKenna..."

"I'm It's so hot."

Holding her, Ray stiffened. Donna McKenna was about to pass out. Her eyes were half-closed, her skin a flushed pink. He put the water bottle to her lips gently. Ray took her all in—airbrushed skin, nice curves, a full head of blonde hair that seemed to be all hers. For a woman in her late forties, she looked remarkable, as if she had discovered the secret to fighting entropy and rubbed it all over herself. Her white dress and gold jewelry gave her a clean appearance that matched her natural, or unnatural, beauty. Ray felt uncomfortable, confused, and slightly turned on. He scooped her up with both arms and carried her to the cruiser, still running, and laid her in the back seat.

Jerry came trotting up. He leaned into the back seat and felt her pulse, her forehead. "Mrs. McKenna."

No response.

"What happened?" Jerry's eyes said *oh no, oh no, oh no.*

"I was doing a walk around, and she just appeared. She must have broken off from the governor without anyone noticing. I gave her some water, then brought her to the car."

"I think we need to take her to the emergency room. Don't you think?"

"No," said Mrs. McKenna, her eyes suddenly open. "I want to go to the house. Take me there. Please."

Ray and Jerry passed the same thought back and forth. They couldn't tell her what to do, and neither wanted to talk to the governor.

"Officer, please," her voice now smooth and direct, "Philip knows I can't take the heat. He'll be just fine without me."

Then Mrs. McKenna looked directly into Ray's eyes, put her hand on his bicep, and squeezed gently. Ray felt a small electric probe stick him somewhere very pleasant.

"And then I'd like this nice officer who helped me to drive me home. I hope that's okay."

"Okay."

For a lot of reasons, Ray was happy to drive her to Chilmark. He got behind the wheel, chewing his lip to keep from smiling. He had a gorgeous woman in his back seat. He had air conditioning. As he turned toward County Road, the crunching of the wheels on the crushed stone seemed deafening, but only a few people turned their heads for a moment to watch him drive away.

The McKennas had a house in Chilmark—up-island, as locals called it. On Martha's Vineyard, the rich lived in town. The out-of-sight rich lived in the woods up-island, where they can't be found for a few weeks a year. The towns of West Tisbury, Chilmark, and Gay Head (recently renamed Aquinnah) were about as accessible as a stuck door. The towns had few residents and even fewer reasons to go there. A general store that doubled as a post office and a chocolate shop in a tiny house that hired special needs kids was the extent of it. (Word caught on about the chocolate place, and it became a tourist magnet for bleeding-heart do-gooders.) For a few weekends a year, the Agricultural Hall set up farm stands to sell fifteen-dollar-a-jar honey, hemp baskets, and earthenware bowls to tourists who ventured up in Range Rovers. There was absolutely nothing exotic or glamorous about being up-island. It was a wool sock in a Birkenstock sandal.

The McKennas were able to get several acres with water access between two natural preserves for an unheard of two million dollars with a rider of a four-million-dollar donation to the Land Bank and Sierra Club. The governor's family immigrated to the US three generations ago and started a logging business in Western Massachusetts. Four million was just enough to keep the ecologists, the preservationists, and the neighbors quiet as long as no one stepped on the dune grass. Four million was the entry fee to summer in up-island seclusion with the rest of the out-of-sights.

The McKenna house on its several acres with water access was stately and gray, identical to the other stately gray houses with water access on several acres. Only an old metal mailbox announced its presence to the public. About a half mile down the road, wooden gates gave the impression visitors weren't wanted, even when they stood open.

Ray was on the dirt road of the McKenna house. Donna McKenna was quiet in the back seat. She had been for the past twenty minutes, patting her chin absently while staring out the window. Ray hadn't attempted any conversation. He was lost in a thought of his own—that she looked preoccupied, and no longer in need of help. Her recovery from the heat was swift.

"You can stop here," she announced suddenly, as though she'd just realized where she was.

They'd passed through the gates but were still several hundred yards from the main house. Ray didn't like the idea of dropping her off in the woods, in the heat, and then getting called out for it after the helpless woman display at the golf club.

"Mrs. McKenna, we're almost there. I'll drop you off in front."

"No. I don't want to…Just let me walk a bit. I feel much better." She added, "If anyone asks, I'll say I in-sisted and you drove me as far as I would let you."

Ray stopped the car. Twisting, he put his arm over the back of the seat bench and looked at her. She had her hand back on her chin, gazing out at something. Before he could protest, she opened the door and stepped out. He watched her walk up the road, turn a corner, and she disappeared into the trees, the same way she had come into his life.

CHAPTER 3
DEATH AND DIAMONDS

"JESUS H. CHRIST."

It was about eight in the morning, too early to go bear hunting or whatever Jerry dragged Ray out of bed for that morning. He had called him early, at seven. "You on the schedule today, Ray? We got a call to check out a noise in the woods." And they climbed into a van with animal-trapping equipment, only the humane type, of course, and drove up-island to look for something that was probably gone hours ago. Ray had dozed on the drive up, letting his mind wander to the girls in tiny shorts scooping ice cream, Mrs. McKenna in the back seat of the cruiser, becoming an over-achieving cyclist sprinting up hills to the Gay Head cliffs. They had gotten out of the van approximately where the noise was reported, each with a neck-loop contraption to drop over the beast's head, and Ray realized he had no idea how to use the thing. A gun, yes. Taser, yes. This thing that looked like a belt on the end of a stick, no. *How hard could it be? Are bears any more difficult than crackheads?*

"Jesus H. Christ," repeated Jerry, louder.

Ray imagined rabbits gutted, a deer's neck slashed by huge claws, the thing still breathing. A hundred yards away, he saw Jerry crumple next to a boulder, fall to his knees. *Something's not right.* Ray started running, his pulse quickened, and then he saw two faces: Jerry's and a dead woman's.

She had bulging eyes as if the lids had been peeled back or cut off, and her slack mouth was crusted with a white foam. She was a middle-aged woman, tawny gray hair, thin but not fit, dressed in full Indian garb of calf-high leather moccasins, beaded vest, bird feathers on clips. She was very dead, had been for hours, and a rope tied her to a boulder to keep her from falling to the ground. The letters *M-O-S-H-U-P* were crudely painted on the boulder above her head. There were no signs of struggle, exterior wounds, or even any blood on the woman. There was no sign anyone else had been there. Ray ran through his homicide mental manual and chewed his lip while he was thinking.

Jerry, still on his knees, hurled up his cookies. Ray took out his phone to do a bit of research.

"Moshup…is, like, an Indian god," Ray muttered. "Folklore says he created the Vineyard with his giant hands. Like molding clay."

"Whatever the hell it is, it's messed up." Jerry sounded scared, and angry. "This kind of stuff doesn't happen around here. It just doesn't. I'm going to call the hospital to send over an ambulance to get her out of here before anyone else comes by."

"No, wait," Ray said. "Don't do anything. Don't touch anything. I mean, it looks messed up because it's all a show, obviously. I've seen cases like this where the whole thing has been staged to say something. Or have people believe something."

"Like what?"

"I don't know. I'm just pretty sure this woman has been drugged, and she's obviously dressed up and tied to this rock with a big message written across it. She might have staged this and it's a suicide. Possibly. Or someone did this to her and went through a lot of trouble to make sure we got a message."

Ray could feel in his gut there was something very odd about the crime. Jerry stared at him, his face blank as an empty holster. Ceremonial killings of Indians were not common on the island. No kind of violent crime was. Ray's big-city experience suddenly put him in the driver's seat, and he wanted to go a very specific direction.

After a long minute, Jerry asked, "What should we do?"

"Call Boston PD."

Discreetly, Ray snapped a picture of the woman and texted it to his mother.

Do you know who this is?

———————•••———————

Two hours later, another small plane landed at the airport, carrying a forensics team from Boston. There was no press or public hanging around the gate this time. No one paid attention to the large metal suitcases rolling across the tarmac. The team climbed into SUVs, drove quietly to the crime scene, dropped their cases on the ground without a word, snapped on latex gloves.

Ray had seen enough bodies in his time that he could figure it within a few hours, and right now, he was betting she had been dead before four that morning. They'd found her at eight, and she looked cool but not totally stiff. More than four hours was what he would bet, if he was a betting man, which he was.

In a white jumpsuit, the examiner leaned over the body.

"Time ten twenty-four a.m. Victim is female between the ages of forty-five and fifty-five. No visible signs of struggle or assault. No external wounds. The skin color and constriction of pupils indicates a high probability of narcotics. Estimated time of death is six to eight hours prior as indicated by loss of heat from the body, accounting for an air temperature of eighty-four degrees, as well as the passage of the primary flaccidity phase."

Ray couldn't help but smile. That put it between two and four.

The examiner pushed pause on his iPhone and addressed Jerry.

"Are you the senior officer that found the body?"

"I am."

"Is this exactly as you found it?"

"Yes. We were called at six-thirty a.m. Someone thought they heard a disturbance in the woods. Seemed kind of a long drive, but we were the only officers available, and I brought a backup guy we've hired for the summer. We walked around a while, and then I found her. Just like that."

The examiner's gloved hand lifted the woman's leg and ran up her thigh. "The areas which are in contact with the ground are not discolored by blood pooling in the interstitial tissues, indicative of the victim dying here. My estimate is she was placed here in a drugged state and then administered a lethal dose of something. We'll run a full autopsy in the lab. Be glad we're in Massachusetts, or you wouldn't get one on a Native American."

Jerry stood back a few feet, fidgeting.

"Do you have an ID?" asked the examiner.

"You mean…for her?"

"Yes, the deceased."

Jerry was in the deep end of the pool, drowning.

"Busick will be here in a minute. He's already briefed the governor." And with that, the examiner was done.

Tom Busick worked with Ray's boss, Peter Boyer, which meant he would know about the voluntary leave and sideline Ray sooner or later. Tom was an asshole, which meant it would be sooner, as in, as soon as he showed up. The man would piss all over this case and call it his, as he held all the cards, and then Ray would be reading parking meters for the rest of the summer.

The first island murder case since the landing of Bartholomew Gosnold, with the governor down the road no less, and Ray standing five feet from the stiff that could put his career back on track. But Busick…anyone but Busick. Ray needed an ace, a lever, anything to not get kicked aside.

Within a few minutes, a black Escalade pulled up to the now makeshift parking lot. Ray's nemesis swung open the heavy door and took his time getting out. He wore khakis shorts, Teva sandals, a too-tight polo stretched over an enormous gut like a snake swallowing a volleyball. His bald head glittered with sweat. This was the retired baseball coach coming back to set the rookies straight.

He slammed the door and walked up in less than a hurry, spraying a thick Boston accent into the phone. Ray could tell by the kissy word choice that the governor was on the other end.

Jerry went up to Busick and stuck out his hand. Busick walked right past.

"Scotty, what cha got for me?"

The forensic examiner had cleaned up his instruments, put away his samples, labeled his baggies, and locked up his case. He still had his latex gloves on.

"It's what you see, Tom. Probably a cocktail of narcs, but we'll bag her and I'll call you in a few days."

"Do we have a time?"

"Between two and four this morning."

"Who found her?"

Jerry spoke up. "We did. Tisbury police. We got a call around six-thirty that there might be a disturbance in the woods, so we came up…"

Ray's phone buzzed in his pocket. His mother had texted him back.

That's Nora Winnetukqet.

What's wrong with her?

I think she's been drugged

Is she dead?????

*I'm at an active crime scene.
Don't share this picture with anyone*

Yes that's Nora. I saw her last week.

Ray slipped the phone back in his pocket.

"Do you have an ID?" Busick smiled at Jerry like he was a toddler.

"Not yet."

"Did you, uh, follow up with the person who phoned in the disturbance?"

Ray interrupted. "The body is Nora Winnetukqet. Pretty sure."

"Pretty sure, huh?" Busick turned around. "Been a long time, Ray. Heard you were on disability."

"Just leave."

"Uh-huh. How, uh, do you know Ms. Winnie-the-Pooh here?"

"My family has a house on the island. We know a lot of locals."

Busick folded his arms and widened his stance. "So you got a shack on Paradise Island. I would have invited myself over for boat drinks if I knew you were so *posh*."

"Next time, Tom. Right now, it's like Jerry said—we got out here and it was exactly as you see. Staged for an audience."

"Interesting. So, you think all of this is to send a message? What's the message?"

"Well, she's Indian. Moshup is Indian folklore. Maybe she was put out here as a warning sign to others."

"Looks like we've got ourselves an injun expert."

Busick walked around to the other side of the boulder. The body was now gone, zipped in a plastic bag and gurneyed to the back of a car. A few people in jumpsuits were picking through the grass with long steel tongs.

Busick went into commando mode.

"I want a report from every neighbor within five miles who might have seen or heard something. I want a full list of the victim's relatives, what she did, who she saw, where she went in the past few months. I want to know how much money she had and who gains from her death. I want to know specifically if she had anything to do with the governor's office."

He paused. "You guys don't get much action here, I know. So, let me do the thinking, and then we can get back to enjoying our summer. I told the governor I would brief him today and every day until this is resolved. You guys gotta dig something up ASAP."

Busick walked back to the Escalade and drove off.

"What a jerk," muttered Jerry.

"Yup."

———————•••———————

Ray's phone kept buzzing all the way back to the station, so he turned it off. When he got into the Volvo, he turned it back on and saw fourteen texts from his mother. She'd gotten the gold star for ID-ing Nora so quickly, so Ray gave her a pass for the relentless follow-up.

When he turned down Juniper Lane, he could see her standing on the porch. She didn't even wait for him to park the car in the garage but came right up to the window.

"Ray, what the hell is going on?"

"Let me park, Ma. I'll tell you."

On the porch, Anne had two iced teas and a bottle of bourbon, open and dented. "I saw Nora about a week ago. I looked at your picture and I couldn't believe it. Where were you?"

"Ma, what I'm going to tell you cannot be repeated. No one knows except a few people at Tisbury Police and

Boston PD. The governor knows too. It appears Nora was drugged and killed. We don't know who, or really how. She was tied to a boulder, you saw how she was dressed up, and someone painted 'Moshup' on it. It looked very theatrical."

"Dear Lord. Poor Nora. But you know, I knew something was strange about her."

"What do you mean?"

"You know, she was nice enough to me, but she had a real vicious streak. Some people couldn't get along with her. And then there was a crazy thing with her husband. Ran off and left her years ago. Turned out to be a big shot in politics, I think. But they didn't get divorced, just moved apart. Real strange if you ask me. I saw her last in line at Cronig's. We said hello. You know me, I talk to everyone."

"How was she? Do you remember anything unusual?"

"Oh, she always had some cause or another. Kill the people so the animals can live."

"Did she have friends or family who are Native Americans?"

"Well, she's part Indian, of course, and she's related to, oh, whatshisname up there that's championing the whole casino thing—Mathias. She didn't like the tribe being so aggressive. She didn't like people in general, which is why her husband left her. How can you be in politics and have a wife who hates everyone?"

"Who is this husband who didn't divorce her? Is he still in politics?"

Anne pulled a leg up close to her chest and leaned back in her chair. She put a hand on her kerchiefed head and sucked on her teeth.

"Oh Christ, what's his name. Good-looking guy."

"It wasn't Winnetukqet?"

"No, no. That's *her* name. His was something else. It was so long ago. I don't think your father and I knew the guy except through someone mentioning he went off to Boston to do…Ammons. That's it. Henry Ammons. You believe I remembered that?" Anne laughed.

Ray took out his phone and looked up Henry Ammons, quickly finding a current listing of him as the governor's chief campaign manager for his reelection campaign.

"So it looks like this Ammons guy is now running the governor's campaign."

"You're kidding. Isn't he on the island right now? Didn't they all get here the other day? Go get the *Times* and the *Gazette* out of the living room."

Top of the fold of both papers were pictures of the governor and his wife exiting the plane, doing their signature human *W*, and behind them the entourage of family and staff. Anne put out her hand.

"Get me my magnifying lens."

The two of them looked closely at each picture. The captions were useless. The story didn't call out the staffers by name, just that they had arrived for the governor's annual vacation, blah, blah. Ray looked up the stories online, but there wasn't anything different about the digital editions. Then he did a search for pictures of Henry Ammons and found a few.

"Ma, take a look. This picture online and this one of the guy in the plane door look similar."

"You're right, that could be him."

"So if he's here, then he's gotta know about Nora's death. The governor's office knows, so Ammons must have found out. Whether they know he was married to Nora Winnetukqet or not is unclear. If they know and haven't said anything, then they're trying to cover up the connection. If they don't know, then it's up to Ammons to make a move. Either way, the governor's office has to make a statement, and either act surprised or not. Ma, this is huge…"

Ray could feel his spine tingling. He was onto something that would make Busick's mouth water like a dog on a leash with the food six inches in front of him. He poured himself a bourbon and tea and downed the whole thing.

"All right," he continued, "so why Nora? What's she done to someone, or what does she know or not know that she knows, and why now when the governor is here, like it's part of the staging?"

"Woooow." Anne was still looking through the magnifying lens at the picture in the *Times*. "Check that out. I bet you that's five, maybe six carats."

An up-close picture showed Donna McKenna's left hand with a diamond ring the size of a regulation basketball. If anything that monstrous came through Ray's father's jewelry store, it would never reach the case. Anne would have snatched it up or it would have been chopped into bite-size engagement rings.

"I've never seen a stone that big on anyone. It's gotta be full of flaws."

"You know, I had Donna McKenna as a detail yesterday. I drove her from Farm Neck to their house in Chilmark."

"How did you get that?"

"We were called from the casino meeting to run the governor's party from the airport up-island. I was in the cruiser that escorted the governor and his family to Farm Neck."

"And now we know Henry Ammons came in on the same flight."

"He was, but I didn't know it. When we get to Farm Neck, it's hot as hell and Mrs. McKenna has a heat stroke. Almost into my arms."

"You're kidding me."

"I was walking around doing basic security checks when she came from, like, behind a tree and fainted right into me."

"Did you see her ring?"

"Christ, no. I was too busy looking at her." Ray husked a laugh. "She's very in shape." He could feel his cheeks tighten as he held back a smile.

"Well, you know, these women got all the time in the world to look good."

Anne fingered her diamond earrings and adjusted the kerchief on her head. She was an attractive woman in her late sixties with a strong profile and bright green-blue eyes. She carried herself straight-backed, head up, chin out, neck stretched. There had been a line of suitors before Carl, and like a conveyor belt, the line rumbled back to life after he died.

"So, anyway, we drive thirty-plus minutes, just her and me in the cruiser, not saying a word, up to their place in Chilmark, and then she demands that I only drive her halfway to the house. I thought, you just had a heat stroke and now you want to walk in the sun? But she insisted, so I let her out and turned back to Farm Neck."

Anne hugged her knee harder and poured herself another iced tea and bourbon mix. "From the thirty seconds you've told me, it sounds like Mrs. McKenna gets off the plane, goes to the event with her husband, fakes a heat stroke to get out of it, has you, a guy in a uniform she doesn't know and can get hard-headed with if she wants, drive her to all the way to Chilmark, before getting out to walk through the woods with that big diamond ring on. So why doesn't she want anyone to know she's coming up to the house? That's what I wanna know."

"Sure, Donna McKenna hates her overambitious husband and wears big jewelry. Who cares! The first murder on Martha's Vineyard since Gosnold mowed down the Indians just happened! Christ, it's been hours. Where the hell is the statement?"

Ray checked the governor's press page on his phone to see if a statement had been issued. He hadn't received any updates or texts from either the Tisbury or Boston PD, nor his contracting company, SES. Dead silence. The body was on a plane for Boston. Busick was probably on his hourly phone call with the governor's office doing his best "I'll get it done" impression. Jerry DeBettencourt was home with a sore ass. Henry Ammons was either shitting a brick or working up crocodile tears.

Ray felt he could be on top of the mountain if he had a firm story on Nora. The pieces were moving quick.

The July afternoon turned into a cool evening. A weather pattern that couldn't make up its mind between an annoying mist and a dripping faucet curled a lazy tail over the Cape and Islands and didn't move. Ray spent the rest of the night waiting for news that didn't materialize. Like the heavy, gray clouds that wouldn't break, someone very high up the food chain was holding a gag over Nora's death. Ray had a shopping list of suspicions. So did his mother who, in neat cotton socks, putted around the house, calling out items to add to the list, as if Ray, the over-eager secretary, were writing them all down. The more tea she drank, the more she was convinced that Donna McKenna and that damn ring were part of this.

"I bet you her husband is a pushy bastard. He gave her that ring to say, 'You're mine, and everyone is going to know it.'" She clapped her hands in the air like trapping a moth. "That's what you call a bird in a cage. Or a dog with a diamond collar."

Anne's musings floated in the air above Ray's mind. He wasn't completely blind to the signal flare that was Donna McKenna. She looked good. It had been a long, long time for Ray, and lots of women looked good. But she looked really good.

His mother broiled a salmon soaked in butter, garlic, basil, thyme, oregano, white wine. The two of them ate at the wooden kitchen table with more wine, gabbing theories when their mouths weren't full, and when they were. Around nine that night, Ray's phone rang in his pocket. It was Jerry. Ray pressed to answer before it finished the first ring.

Jerry sounded both annoyed and amused, a common reaction to dealing with off-island temperaments.

"Who's this guy Busick? He's been on me all night."

"Ha. What does he want?"

"Well, he's had me digging around in county records for hours. Would you know, Ms. Winnetukqet was married to a guy named Henry Ammons in Tisbury in 1990, and what's more, Ammons is working as the governor's campaign manager. He's here on the island. I couldn't believe it. He and Nora separated but didn't ever divorce. I got a hold of some county records. Shows she had utilities in her name about ten years ago, so I'm guessing that's when he left. Took me to hell and back again to find that out."

"Nicely done, Jerry." Ray tried to sound surprised. "Did Nora have a will? A house and land is worth something around here. Maybe she's got something tucked away too."

"Yeah, that's a dinger. Can't find one yet, but that doesn't mean there isn't one. Checked MV Law, even called her bank to see if she had a safe deposit box, but apparently she doesn't."

"Who's doing a search of her premises? You need to look in the house for evidence. And a will. You gotta start there."

"It's a funny thing, Ray. I said the same thing to Busick, and he said that they would 'get around to it.'"

"So no one's gone there yet?"

"I didn't go."

Ray chose his next words very carefully. "As part of evidence collection, Jerry, you have to go. It could get a lot of answers."

"What about Busick? Maybe he'll go if you tell him. Didn't you guys work together?"

"This is a Dukes County case. You have jurisdiction. Don't let him push you around. If he gets up your ass about it, tell him that you didn't like waiting so long to investigate the premises. There could be evidence material to the case that no one is picking up. If you keep waiting, you're giving the perp potentially more time to go back and cover his tracks."

Ray was planting a seed so huge in Jerry's brain, it stuck out like a tumor. It was a gamble to circumvent the Boston PD, but he had procedure to fall back on. If Busick called him out, he could pull the material evidence card, which was still a spin of the wheel. The man wouldn't want to be caught sleeping on the job given his let's-get-this-wrapped-up-before-Labor-Day speech. Ray's mind began to swirl thinking about what could be in Nora's house right now. He wanted to stop and think through why no one had gone there yet, but the desire to go himself was much, much stronger.

"Swing by and get me. I'm on Juniper and Main."

"Okay, Ray. We can drive out there, but if we don't have due cause to go in, we're driving back."

"Sure."

Nora Winnetukqet's small house was still and dark. In the moonlight, it had a creepy witch-in-the-woods feeling. There was no conspicuous yellow crime scene tape or evidence of anyone being there at all.

Jerry pulled the cruiser up to the house and cut the engine. It was dead silent.

"Well, we're here."

Buttressing a weak cop's backbone wasn't Ray's strong suit, so he just got out of the car. The austere salt-box was the house of a recluse. Ray would have laid odds on a vegetable garden and compost pile.

The front door didn't look functional, so they went around back, where they peered into dark windows.

"No one's here. We probably need a warrant."

Ray went for the door, but it was already ajar. Good enough.

"That'll take too long."

Ray stepped into the kitchen, with Jerry cautious as a cat behind him, and flicked on a flashlight. An enormous cast iron stove anchored one side of the kitchen across from a wooden table and chairs. The stove pipe went through the wall to the outside. It seemed to be the primary cooking surface, as there was no oven or microwave. An old white refrigerator hummed louder and louder, then clicked off. Earthenware bowls and cups were stacked precariously in open faced-cabinets. Piles of paper—mail, newspapers, sketches—lay everywhere. It looked like dwarves lived there.

They moved through a hall to the front parlor of the house. There was a heavy fragrance of wood and damp. The floor creaked like an old boat. Ray swept his flashlight around the disheveled parlor. Nora's housekeeping wouldn't make it easy to find anything. As far as he could see, she had no filing system except piling papers on every surface.

Ray moved up the stairs to the second floor. The roof pitched hard on both sides, leaving room for only two small bedrooms and one bath. The first bedroom was a mess with more papers, clothes, and boxes. The other was surprisingly neat. The bed was made, with a quilt folded in half. Two prim dressers flanked either side. No dust on the bureau. Ray's mind started to churn. *Someone is playing clean up.*

He snapped on a glove and turned on a side lamp. He opened drawers and peeled back layers of more papers, clothes, pictures. Nora had years of clippings without a clear theme: news of the local Wampanoag tribe meetings, an editorial on preserving wren habitats on State Beach, protests about expanding the Stop and Shop. Superficially, the room had been smoothed over, but what for? He looked under the bed, in the corners of the room, moved the dressers from the wall. Nothing.

Next, the bathroom, which had a tight shower and a few shelves, along with a medicine cabinet above the sink. He pulled the chain above the mirror and opened it. Old aspirin bottles, Band-Aids, a rusty razor. Nora had no taste for the feminine, that was clear—Ray couldn't even find a hairbrush.

He closed the cabinet and was reaching for the light chain to turn it off when he spotted something behind the base of the sink, something that sparkled like a forgotten Christmas ornament. He bent down, and before he picked it up, he knew what it was.

Donna McKenna's engagement ring. The ring with a diamond the size of a yacht surrounded by sapphires fixed to a thick gold band. His mother was right. It was five carats or more, easily the biggest stone he'd ever seen that close, bigger than anything that ever came into his father's jewelry store. It glittered with self-indulgence. Ray understood how it might keep a bird happy in its cage, or a dog tame on a leash. He put the ring in his pocket and pulled the light chain.

Footsteps came up the creaky stairs. Jerry's flashlight swung around and landed on Ray.

"Find anything?"

Ray clenched his jaw and put his hand in his pocket.

"I sure didn't," Jerry sighed. "This place is a mess. I was hoping you were right and there would be something here. I'm going to have to file a report that we came by."

Ray exhaled. He pulled the ring out of his pocket and held it in Jerry's flashlight. It fractured the light into a galaxy of stars on their faces.

"Would you look at that," Jerry whispered.

Ray studied Jerry's face to see if two and two were making four.

"Where did you find that?"

"On the bathroom floor."

"It must be an antique, an heirloom, or maybe her ex-husband Henry gave it to her a long time ago."

Two and two were just about making three and a half, so Ray carried it the last yard.

"I don't think it's hers, so I suggest we report it as evidence. Let's bag it up and get going."

———————

On the drive back, Ray kept his hands on his lap and forced himself to make small talk about the case. After a while, he leaned his head back and zoned out to the headlights curving slowly along the road, to the memory of Donna McKenna when she lay in his arms, light as a cheerleader, her hair falling over her face.

Later that night, Ray lay in bed with a busy mind. The blinds were up, and the moon bent through the window with its mien of thoughtfulness. He put his hands behind his head and went over and over what there was to go over. Nora, basically a female hobbit, the estranged wife of the governor's campaign manager and part Wampanoag, was either dressed up, or convinced to dress up, in Indian garb before being drugged and killed. She was tied to a rock and someone wrote the word "Moshup," which had a direct link to the Native Americans who lived here before the English arrived. The Wampanoag tribe was bitterly divided over the building of a bingo parlor on the island, as were many islanders, and no happy resolution was in sight.

Then the governor lands on the island for his summer of fundraising, and his wife does her heat stroke bit and dips out of the golf club. She asks to be taken home, but not all the way, and then her engagement ring turns up at Nora's house, at maximum one day after she and the governor arrived. And now, a full day after the discovery of Nora's body, there still is no statement from the governor's office regarding the connection between Henry Ammons and his estranged wife. In fact, there's been no news about Nora's death at all.

Ray closed his eyes and turned over. A vision of Donna minus her white dress clouded his thoughts.

CHAPTER 4
FISHING IS A LIVING, SOMETIMES

MIRRORED OAKLEYS FASTENED WITH A neon wet strap, camo cargo shorts, running shoes with no socks, tanned Tasmanian Devil tattoo—Andrew was taking a day off from playing bad-news building inspector to go fishing. Alone. Man against nature.

The thirty-five-foot Donzi ZF sport fishing boat with two Yamaha outboard motors, named *Alley Kat*, revved her engines, still docked in Lobsterville Beach marina. With fresh bait in the cooler, poles strapped to the stern, a twelve-pack of beer, and cold fried chicken, she was set. July's waters through the Elizabeth Islands and the Atlantic side of the island were prime for catching bonitos—silver six-pounders known for their speed. One generous summer, Andrew had caught eight bonitos in a single trip. To commemorate man's spot at the top of the food chain, he had a tiger cat wearing a sombrero holding a bottle of hot sauce biting into a flailing fish painted on the side of the boat.

Andrew tapped on his GPS, and the blue light of the screen cast its hue into the dark cabin. He was scanning for a tuna trawler. Bonitos travel with bigger fish, and commercial outfits had fancy equipment to spot the schools as they ran up and down New England waters. This morning, there were three trawlers out of New Bedford—the *Leroy*, the *JAD*, and the *Apollo Forte*. The *JAD* was the biggest at fifty-two feet, an Alaskan-made '77 Hoquiam schooner with a fiberglass hull, four fish holds, two nets, and a crew of eight under Captain T. S. Whiting. The *JAD* had cast off at 5:30 a.m. from New Bedford harbor, with baited nets and room for a thousand pounds of fish with ice.

Captain Thomas Whiting sipped coffee from a thirty-two-ounce plastic Dunkin Donuts mug, watching flashing radar blips moving south toward Rhode Island, probably following a school of skipjack. If none of the equipment broke, it might be a good day.

He pushed a button, and the deck buzzer signaled the crew to heave and pull, unwinding giant spools of netting that cranked-cranked-cranked down to the dark water.

The nets set on both the starboard and port, the guys would head below to start up the ice machines.

The first haul was light, a few hundred pounds, but keepers. The crew cut and tossed what they couldn't keep, pushing the rest in the fish hole. The nets rolled and cranked for another drop. Whiting looked down on his radar and spotted a fancy thirty-five-footer in his wake, about a quarter mile behind. He picked up the VHF radio.

"*Alley Kat*, this is the *JAD*. *Alley Kat* this is the *JAD*."

"*JAD* this is *Ally Kat*. I'm on channel sixty-eight. Over."

"*Alley Kat*, you're out early. What are you doing back there?"

"Fishing."

"Catch anything?"

"Bonitos. A few of yours."

"I'm trying to make a living. Pull up and drop them off," Whiting laughed into the radio.

"I already threw them back. Not my game."

Whiting was about to ask the *Alley Kat* where she was headed when shouting rose from the deck below. The shrill of a fire alarm overcame the vessel. He cut the engines and slid down the stair rails, lighting the palms of his hands on fire. He turned his key in the alarm bell. Silence.

All eight guys were standing at the rail.

"What? We pick up something?"

Howland, the senior deckhand, spoke. "Cap, look."

He pointed to the net swinging heavily on the arm of the boom, a full catch. Silver tunas flailed against each other in panic, mouthing the dry air, trying to keep alive. Except the one that didn't.

"What the fuck is that?"

A big guy, six feet or more, with a torso like a masticated chicken carcass chewed by a dog down to the off-white bone behind the meat swung in the net. The flesh-stripped face locked in a scream, jaw bones and teeth exposed, had water draining out of dark eye holes. Whiting had never seen a man eaten by the ocean before.

"Whadda we do, Cap?"

"Put it on the deck."

The crank lowered the net. Fish and man carcass splayed over their rubber boots. It was definitely a man— the genitalia were bitten but not gone. Some blue-black patches on an arm where a bit of skin remained seemed to be a faded tattoo.

"Do we call the Coast Guard?"

Whiting rubbed his face vigorously with his hand. "We gotta. I can't believe I fucking fished up a dead guy." He stumbled up the steps. "I can't deal with this shit right now."

Hands shaking, he reached for the VHS intercom, but there was a call already coming through.

"*JAD* this is *Alley Kat*. *JAD* this is *Alley Kat*. What's your status?"

"We fished up some serious shit. I gotta call CG. Over."

Whiting opened up his log book and typed *7:46 a.m., fish haul, body of a man in net. In bad shape. Radioed Coast Guard to come get it.*

At around nine a.m., Ray was in Leslie's pharmacy, leafing through the *Times* and the *Gazette*. Finally, above the fold in both papers, the headlines he was waiting for: "First Suspicious Death on Island in 75 Years" and "Aquinnah Resident Found Dead with Native Reference." Ray scanned for any mention of Henry Ammons and found it buried in paragraph four of one article:

Nora Winnetukqet, longtime island resident and part Wampanoag Indian, was married to Governor McKenna's current campaign manager, Henry Ammons, in 1991. They separated soon after when Mr. Ammons moved back to Boston. Mrs. Winnetukqet legally changed her name in 1996 and remained an island resident. The governor's office released a statement saying Mr. Ammons is "deeply saddened" by this tragedy. They have no children.

Useless, thought Ray. "Deeply saddened" is what you said to your neighbor when their tropical bird escaped in the winter. Then again, Henry and Nora hadn't seen each other for years. Ray tucked in both newspapers and chewed his lip. He put two bucks on the counter and called Jerry at the station.

"Officer DeBettencourt."

"Hey, Jerry, it's Ray."

"Well, you've sure got some timing. You were the next person on my list."

"Oh yeah?"

"Got a call from one of Nora's neighbors. Said people were at her house last night after we left."

Ray stopped midstep. "Who was it?"

"The neighbor making the report doesn't know, but there was enough noise to raise concerns. I sent one of my guys down there as soon as he got in this morning, and he called me back, saying the place was gone over."

Ray's gears turned. "Hey, Jerry, did you write up a report from our trip last night? And did you, by chance, file that evidence?"

"Not yet. I was about to do that this morning, and whaddayaknow, something else popped up. This has been one hell of a summer. I can't remember it ever being this bad."

"What came up?"

"Someone drowned near Cuttyhunk, I guess a few days ago—found by a fishing boat, a real mess. The Coast Guard brought him to the hospital to see if an ID is possible. I checked, and there are no missing persons or lifeguard reports so I'm not sure who he is. He could have been from off-island and floated out. Are you on the schedule?"

"Uh-huh."

"One of my guys is out sick, and I sent Sawyer out already. Can you go to the hospital and get an ID on our Indian."

"Indian?" Ray's brain was now in overdrive. Another dead body, possibly the same tribe, possibly connected to Nora?

"Oh yeah, I didn't tell you. The Coast Guard says he has Indian-looking tattoos, so he could be. Then again, you know, he's been out in the water a few days, so he's in bad shape. Can you figure out where he belongs? We don't have room for another body." Jerry tried to laugh but he sounded exhausted.

"Jerry, I know you're up to your eyeballs so I'll do everything I can. If our floater is connected, we'll figure out how. Let me get the car and I'll be at the hospital in twenty minutes. Oh, and did you see the *Times* and the *Gazette*? The governor's office finally put out a statement about Nora and Henry Ammons."

"I did. Oh yeah, another thing. I got a call from Busick this morning. He wants to know how the investigation is going. I told him we didn't have much but I'd be sending him a report today."

"Did you mention that we went to Nora's house?"

"No. I'm going to send him a full status report as soon as I get it done. Maybe he'll leave me alone for a little bit after that."

Ray snorted. "I doubt it."

———————

Ray made it back in seven minutes. His blood pumped with his quick stride, his mind churning on Henry and Nora, the big fat ring in her hermitage, the governor's reelection, Donna in the heat, the efficacy of narcotics, the Indian god Moshup shaping the island like Play-Doh. Ray knew Nora wasn't a thief—she hadn't stolen the ring or needed the money, which meant it made its way there from a third party, likely the one who cleaned up the bedroom nice, perhaps after it had been used.

The ring had turned up there sometime after Ray dropped off Mrs. McKenna in her driveway and the next evening, when he and Jerry walked through Nora's house. That left not a lot of time for a lot to happen: Nora getting dressed for a tribal dance and pumped with drugs, tied to an Indian landmark, all while her bedroom was used and cleaned up.

On top of that, a John Doe floater brought in by the Coast Guard.

Anne was out on the porch, fanning herself with a grocery circular.

"Did you get my rub-offs?"

Ray let out an exasperated sigh. "I'm sorry, Ma, I got there and then I called Jerry, and I totally forgot. I did get the papers. Look, Nora is on the front page of both."

His mother dropped the flyer and studied both pictures. "I can't believe it," she said. "First island murder in decades. Just when you think you've left all that behind, it comes right up again."

"Separately, I need to use the car this morning to go down to the hospital. The Coast Guard found a guy who drowned near Cuttyhunk. Jerry asked me to see if I can make an ID. He thinks he's an Indian because he has some tattoos."

"Another dead Indian?"

"What? You think it's related?"

"Of course they're related! How many Indians do you think there are around here? They're all from some big chief who had ten wives." She picked up the circular and fanned herself. "Of course they're related. Right now, they happen to hate each other. Let me see those papers again." Anne turned the pages, searching. "Nothing about the casino. I hate the idea, don't you? I want this island to be peaceful, without that trash. I wouldn't be surprised if Mathias got bumped off, now that we're killing Indians."

"You know, Ma, I'm glad you're not on Twitter."

"Oh, don't you kid me. I'm just saying what other people are thinking."

"I'll be back in a few hours." Ray leaned in and kissed her cheek.

"Go. Just make sure you get my rub-offs on the way back."

⸺⸺⸺ ••• ⸺⸺⸺

Ray pulled up to the Martha's Vineyard Hospital, a recently renovated, top-drawer facility off Beach Road in Oak Bluffs. It was the first and largest building after crossing the bridge between a lagoon and Vineyard Haven harbor, though it remained hidden from the road by huge hydrangea bushes. It could have been a sweet little hotel, but pass through the swishing glass doors and there was high-speed Wi-Fi, low-slung couches, and white gloss floors gleaming hygienically in the sunlight from skylights above.

The reception desk was empty. Curious, Ray leaned over to see what was behind it. Then he heard a voice he had heard before.

"Can I help you?"

Ray turned to stare right into Rachel's gorgeous green eyes. Her dark hair was pulled up in a loose bun, and she wore a white coat, open, with all the right curves underneath.

"Uh, yes. I need to ID a body. I'm with the Tisbury police. Don't you work at Dr. Spahr's office?"

"I do. Three days a week, when he's busy, and then I'm here a few days. Your mother is a patient of Dr. Spahr's. I remember when you came in."

Ray's face split to a big, stupid, jack-o-lantern grin. A bonfire of endorphins scorched his brain. Rachel, he guessed, was slightly more than half his age.

"You do? Good memory. You should be a cop. We could use some smart people like you." Ray was about to punch himself for being such a sap.

"Who did you want to see?" She traced a pencil through her hair.

"A John Doe came in from the Coast Guard. Possibly a drowning. From what I hear, he was in bad shape. I'm looking to make an ID."

"Oh, I saw him. It's totally gross. Here, fill out these forms, and I need to see your police badge. Then take the elevator down to Recoveries, room 200."

"I'm not a cop. I mean I am, but…I'm part-time…for now."

"Oh."

She was out of his league, anyway.

The basement smelled of bleach. A small window cut a slit in the door to room 200. Ray knocked and then tried the handle. Locked. After a few seconds, a pair of glasses on a round, bald face appeared in the window, looking skeptical. The door opened a few inches.

"What do you want?" The medical examiner looked like Mr. Magoo.

Ray held up the receipt giving him clearance to view the corpse.

"It's over here," he monotoned.

At the end of the metal tables lay the John Doe. Ray folded down the sheet to a grotesque and bloated corpse stripped down like leftover chicken dinner. He winced and coughed as his stomach turned over.

Magoo paid no attention. "Male, age twenty-two to twenty-five, Native American, possibly asphyxiated in the water. Massive loss of epidermal and muscular tissue caused by one-to-five-inch diameter bites with sharp teeth. No sign of mechanical injuries from a propeller. Estimated time in water forty-eight to seventy-two hours. My guess, very deep sea water. Skeletal impacts appear to be at a minimum. We're running his dentals for a match, which will take a few weeks."

"So you don't know if he drowned?"

"He may have." Magoo was annoyed. "Who sent you?"

"Tisbury."

"Summer hire?"

"Yeah."

"Summer people cause all the problems around here."

CHAPTER 5
THE CAT'S TONGUE

RACHEL ADMIRED HERSELF IN THE bathroom mirror. In a matching black lace brassiere and panties she bought thinking of Dennis, she traced lightly over the seams of the lace, thinking about how nuts it would make him later, how she loved making him nuts until he grunted like an animal. The fury and passion had been there from the day she interviewed at his office. She could feel his stare lingering on her too long, his questions turning personal. She had the job and a dinner date for that weekend after his family had gone back to Maine, when his summer cottage would be empty. It was passion and fire from the first moment, and in two months it hadn't even flickered.

She dipped into a jewelry case and chose dangling peridot earrings because they matched her eyes, because Dennis had commented about how good she looked in jewels and nothing else, because she was the green-eyed goddess that purred at his touch, that scratched his itch like the sandpapery lick of a cat's tongue.

Her phone buzzed.

Be outside in 10. Can't wait
to see you, gorgeous.

Rachel shivered in anticipation, slipped into a black chiffon jumper that was tight at the waist, letting the straps fall down over her shoulders. With her hair down she looked her age, twenty-two, just old enough to be away from home but still feel she was living under its protective coating. Rachel had dated many men, some married, but Dennis was different. He told her on their second date she was all that mattered. They would cruise to Bermuda after the season was over. He would help her find a place in the city where they could see each other often. He could help her get into nursing school at his alma mater.

Rachel's roommate stepped into the bathroom, gave a sidelong glance, leaned on the door jam.

"Where's Dr. Moneybags taking you tonight?"

"Someplace very French. Very private." Rachel applied lipstick.

"You know, he's got a wife and three kids. You don't see them, but they exist."

"I know. We've already discussed it. Besides, he's going to buy the tickets next week for our cruise, so he's going to have to take care of it soon."

The roommate rolled her eyes, sighed, and waved goodbye. Rachel airkissed the mirror and walked down to the street.

The Audi RS5 in phantom gray with tinted windows idled under a street lamp. Rachel bounced in high heels over to the door, swung it wide and slid inside, right over to Dennis's lap. She kissed him, bit him on the neck, hungry. Dennis put the RS5 in gear and hit the accelerator too hard. The car jerked out. Rachel put her hands up through the moonroof and laughed.

Le Chambre was on the second floor of a manor house in Tisbury, set back from the road. Jean Macron of Lyon, France, had started the restaurant in the 1980s with four ingredients: butter, garlic, cream, and white wine. Nearly impossible to find, the restaurant had no sign, no overture of welcome to passersby. It was an old-money hideout, not because of the cooking, but because Jean was very French and very discreet. Old money liked discretion. Old money never asked a question that could be politely avoided. Old money drank at the West Chop tennis club until eight o'clock, got in separate cars, and met at the same restaurant for dinner. Le Chambre was a necessary outpost for old money to leave the comfort of their houses without the threat of seeing anyone they didn't know.

Dennis escorted Rachel through the corridor to the second floor. Several parties stood near the entrance to the dining room, eyeing the couple with speaking looks. Rachel squeezed his hand.

"Two for dinner," said Dennis.

"*Pardon, monsieur, notre dîner est plein ce soir,*" replied the hostess as she shook her head. "We are very full."

Dennis dropped Rachel's hand and pointed to the kitchen. "Go in there and tell Jean 'the doctor' is here."

The hostess left her post without changing expression, swung through the kitchen doors, and came out a few seconds later.

"*Monsieur, mademoiselle...s'il vous plaît.*"

The couple was seated in the middle of the restaurant. Rachel became a colorful floor show for the fogged-vision patrons searching for their escargot tongs. Two waiters came over and with a tight bow spoke soft French words while uncorking the wine.

"I'm starved, what about you?" Rachel widened her eyes and bit her lip. She leaned across the table and caressed Dennis's hands, massaging his fingers and palms. She looked like a panther in the black jumper, dark hair, and glittering earrings.

They ordered cinnamon carrot puree, creamed spinach, French onion soup, lobster Thermidor, shrimp Pernod with puff potato pastry, bananas flambe. Jean sent out a bottle of Veuve Clicquot champagne and two chocolates on a plate with "*Merci!*" scripted in raspberry compote. Dennis stood the corks on the table.

"Go find a place for these, babe. Add ours to the collection."

Over the decades, old money had indoctrinated Jean into their coterie by leaving corks on the tops of window sills, along exposed rafters and ledges. Dennis watched Rachel cross to the window to place the corks, her lean body pulling at the chiffon jumper, and felt the familiar itch setting in. She took her time crossing back to the table, giving the patrons more show to watch, and Dennis pulled her into his lap and kissed her hard.

"*Pardon, monsieur,* a call for you." A waiter had appeared, bowing tightly.

"My phone is off for a reason."

"Very urgent, *monsieur*."

Rachel sighed, slid into her seat and held onto Dennis's hand as he walked away. She knew there was only one person who would call every restaurant, make the staff stop in the middle of dinner rush to find Dennis, and he would take her call from the kitchen phone—Donna McKenna. Rachel wondered if there was more, but dismissed it. Mrs. McKenna was a hot mess, Rachel could see that a mile away, and Dennis couldn't stand needy women other than as his patients.

"What's the old addict want now?" Rachel sipped her champagne, annoyed.

"She can wait. I have my own addiction only you can fix."

--- • ---

It was close to one o'clock in the morning when the headlights of the RS5 swung around the back of the office. Rachel dozed on the passenger seat in Dennis's car, drunk on booze, butter, and bananas flambe. Donna's white Mercedes was already there in the parking lot. Dennis took out his key and they walked into the office together silently, in the dark, to the examination room. Dennis knew exactly what she wanted. He turned on a small desk lamp, sat on a rolling stool.

"Last time, I gave you a low-grade opioid. You want to re-up for thirty more pills?"

"That doesn't work anymore. It makes me edgy, and when I'm not edgy, I'm exhausted. I just want to stay here and sleep. I feel so much better when I'm here."

Donna lay down on the exam table and closed her mascara-streaked eyes. The thin paper sheet crinkled as her short cocktail dress rode up her thighs. Dennis flipped through some papers and pulled out drawers looking for the Rx pad.

"I'm going to put you on a low-grade amphetamine to help with the anxiety. Start out taking two of these twice a day and see if that helps."

Donna lay silent, her breathing heavy and slow, her face pale despite the evening makeup. Dennis was tempted to let her sleep it off in the exam room. It would keep her from bending around a tree on the way back to Chilmark. But his two options—sleeping on the waiting room couch or leaving her in the office alone overnight—seemed worse. He pulled her to her feet and shoved the Rx paper into her handbag.

"Come on. You'll be missed."

"No, I won't."

She started up her car, slowly backed up and drove off. Her headlights stayed mostly on the road.

CHAPTER 6
HAIL MARY

MATHIAS'S F-150 SPUN DIRT AND gravel as it bounced up the road to the community center. The road was lined with tall Brazilian men, sitting on the flat beds of trucks, in the shade of pine trees and short bushes, leaning on sticks of backhoes. Their deep brown faces rested without expression, like an El Greco painting that Mathias had seen once—blue and somber. They were day-laborers, hired for less than the locals, happy to earn what they could and send the rest home.

He pulled in front, surveying his crew, the power of a blank check in his pocket. Mathias was indifferent to gambling—he thought only of the money. The tribe had exploding drug and alcohol problems, a new school and cultural center that was only half built had idled for years. Each passing month, hundreds of thousands trickled out of the coffers with no way to replenish, like a gushing pipe. Mathias felt it like a tap in his vein, drawing down his energy. Every day the tap drained him more, every day he willed himself to push harder. Other Massachusetts tribes breezed through the casino-permitting process, but Mathias's battle for the same granted rites was mired in high-priced lawyers and White entitlement. He would have more luck building a toll bridge from the mainland.

A man in a suit walked up to the F-150 and leaned in the window.

"Mathias, good to meet you. Henry Ammons. You brought quite the crew today." Henry squinted and looked up at Mathias, a good head taller.

"You bet I did. I'm tired of waiting around. It's been one delay after another 'cause they're afraid of every little thing. I got these guys up here to myself. I don't give a shit anymore." He slammed the truck door.

"Precisely why I'm up here, Mathias. You know the governor is a friend of the tribe, has been for many years. He wants to see you and the Wampanoag people get what is rightfully yours." A diplomatic pause. "But he's also a resident. He's aware how contentious your project is. He's been given advice to distance himself. It's a fine line for him to walk. For all of us to walk. You go rogue on this and he'll have to publicly denounce it. You have to let the process play out. Trust in the system."

Mathias let rip a vicious comeback. "The 'system' has screwed us for hundreds of years. The 'system' is why we live on less than one percent of the land when we used to have it all. The 'system' is for you, not us. I know what the governor is up to. He's moving his chess pieces around, and you guys think I'm going to roll over and take it up the ass like you're doing me a favor. No way." Mathias pushed a finger in Henry's face. Then he turned his back to Henry to admire his building, his Hail Mary pass to a land of hopes and dreams come true, his little palace where he packed them in all season long via a stream of charter buses straight from the ferry. He put an arm around Henry's shoulder and squeezed.

"Let me show you the place," Mathias grinned wide.

The community center was hot as hell. No AC, electric, or running water. Drew Cogswell had called the town utilities services after the tribal meeting, and Mathias was stuck until the permits came through, or a dozen generators.

"I'm going to transform this place. I want wall-to-wall red rugs, ballroom chandeliers, the bingo along here, a raw bar along the back wall. I'm going to keep the island feel and make it like a night club. Maybe do a live band on weekends."

The center was a little less than six thousand square feet. Mathias made it out to be the next Bellagio.

"That's a lot of casino. How are you going to fund it?"

"I've got two loans, one for the equipment and one for the development. They're in the tribe's name."

"Is that how you're paying the guys outside?" Henry sighed, "You know what, it doesn't matter. Just do this right."

"I've heard your name before. Your wife was Nora Winnetukqet, wasn't she?"

"Yes," Henry said flatly.

Mathias's huge mass closed in on Henry. Hard slices of sun from the skylights illuminated his dark skin, black braided hair. The heat made the thick air hard to breathe. Mathias raised his hand and palmed Henry's shoulder.

"Sorry to see that happen to her."

"Nora and I haven't spoken in years."

Mathias curled his long fingers into hooks. "Your car, the one outside...I saw it at her house the other night. Not too many Jaguars up-island."

"What are you saying, Chief? That I knocked off my wife because...because of what...?"

"You were at her house. I saw your car. You walked in the back door and she was inside waiting for you. Then you went upstairs and turned on the light. That's enough for me to know you're lying about the last time you saw her." Mathias held his stare, he was breathing down on Henry, hot air moving between their faces. Then he let go of the claw grip. Henry shook it off and stormed out, pushed wide the double doors, and cursed under his breath. Then immediately came back in.

"Listen, Chief, I don't want a goddamn stone moved until you show me permits and documents with stamps and signatures and fucking embossed town seals saying your chicken box is above board. The governor doesn't want any more problems. And I don't want to have to come here again. Are we clear?"

And he drove off.

———————

It was Monday, so Dr. Spahr's schedule was light. He left the office to Rachel around two o'clock and went to the beach, leaving her with a stack of follow-ups to do. He called her "babe" and blew her a kiss as the door swung closed. Rachel wanted to go with him, imagining the hungry looks she could get in her very small black bikini. But Dennis didn't ask. He was her boss, hot sex or no.

She remained in the office, a good little girl, phoning in restocking orders for rich drug addicts.

Rachel unlocked the cabinets and counted the inventory, then checked it against the patient records. Antidepressants and painkillers went the quickest, and principally to a handful of names in the files, one being Donna McKenna. Dennis had written her a prescription for twenty milligrams of OxyContin starting in June that year for "abdominal pain." *Twenty milligrams for a petite woman is a lot*, thought Rachel. That's what you prescribe after surgery, or for terminal cancer. Maybe it was necessary once and now she couldn't do without. Rachel finished her stock checks, closed the cabinets, shut down her computer, and locked up. She paused on the steps leading down to the parking lot, wanting Dennis to call her from the beach, to hear his voice asking her to wear that black bikini. She imagined him saying, "Pick up some ice on the way, babe, I need it with you around," and then laugh at his smarmy pickup line.

The call didn't come. She leaned on the door, sighed, then put the phone in her pocket.

In the parking lot a familiar white Mercedes was parked, the windows up and engine running. Rachel came down the steps and recognized Donna McKenna behind huge white sunglasses.

"Where is Dr. Spahr?" Her voice was hoarse.

"I'm sorry, he's gone for the day, Mrs. McKenna. Did you have an appointment?"

She said nothing. Her white, drawn face wore no expression as her head drifted down toward the steering wheel, then snapped back up. Finally, she spoke, barely above the hum of the engine.

"Tell him…to answer…his goddamn phone."

Hunched over, she drove off, jerking the car—brake, accelerator, brake. Now Rachel had a reason to call Dennis. She dialed, but he didn't pick up for her either. She sent a text and waited till it showed as delivered. Looking up again, Rachel watched the car amble onto State Road. For the first time in her life, she felt sorry for a beautiful woman.

———

The Mercedes made a Maypole of the double yellow line. Donna faded in and out of the world, her body searching for a chemical balance, swinging from lucidity to grayed-out nothing. She drove for miles, running on muscle memory, sometimes circling back along the same roads, pulling over on the shoulder to nod off, and then punching the pedal when she woke up. No one stopped to ask if she was all right.

Hours later, the car crept up the hill to the Harbor View Hotel in Edgartown, hit the curb, and stalled out. With much effort, she unclenched her stiff fingers from the wheel. The white pantsuit she'd put on that morning was drenched with sweat, her makeup wiped away. The car door swung wide, and she lifted herself like a just-born fawn. Walking up the hill took everything she had left in her body.

"I'm here, Philip," she whispered. "I made it."

Donna reached out desperately for something, someone. She saw the people inside the brightly light Harbor View lobby, drinking cocktails, eating the lobster tail, shrimp, and raw oysters of a deep-pockets fundraiser, the kind Philip excelled at. Philip would present his Donna, the petite Wellesley grad, perfect wife and mother of two handsome boys, the embodiment of selflessness and support, to complete his persona. Philip and Donna, the second coming of Camelot's Kennedys. *"This is how you win elections,"* he told her. *"Hold your breath. It lets other people relax, and when people relax they vote for you."* Donna closed her eyes and heard his voice in her head pressing her to keep climbing the hill, to just hold her breath one more time because this was his moment. *This is how to win, Donna. Don't be the weak link.* "I'm here, Philip. Please, help…I'm strong too."

Her knees buckled and her body hit the ground. She felt no pain, being completely numb and unable to move or talk, while the world around her swirled. She heard faraway voices, vibrations, hands touched her and rolled her over. She saw Philip's face over her with a sunburst halo of colors all around him, and she tried to smile. He looked disgusted. "You're high, aren't you?"

Henry jogged over and stood by Philip's side, then knelt down in the grass.

"Let me take her to the hospital," Henry whispered. Philip was looking back at the guests and then snapped his head around.

"Hell no. Call the ambulance and I'm going with her. Then get your ass back in there and make sure no one leaves." Addressing the guests, Philip went into crisis control mode. "She's okay, everyone. She's just exhausted. All this campaigning…it would kill any of us."

Donna gazed up at Philip and Henry like her guardian angels. Then she felt herself being lifted into a little bed, the bed floating up and into the sky.

"Someone dumped a load of shit on that party."

Mathias was in the Harbor View bar. He had a clear view of the action on the lawn, the ambulance coming and going, the fundraiser guests in the lobby being soothed over with cocktails and piano music. Smug, he turned to the bartender and finished his drink.

"You're not here for the governor's shindig?" the bartender, probably a summer kid, pattered while polishing a goblet.

"The governor should be paying me to show up. I'm doing him the biggest favor of his career. He puts on this big show about helping native people on the island. Really? Then why's it so hard to get some piece-of-shit permits?"

Mathias motioned for another whiskey. A summer breeze puffed through the French doors of the hotel, and beyond the French doors a wooden deck spanned, full of swaying rocking chairs. Sailboats lazed through Edgartown harbor, the chrome on yachts winked silvery in the setting sun. It was a million-dollar view, the kind that sold dreams of early retirement, beachfront property for those who could afford it, postcards and T-shirts for those who couldn't.

"People see what they want to see," Mathias said. "They see how beautiful the island is, and they think there can't be anything wrong." He got up slowly from the stool and put a five-dollar tip on the bar.

"You working here for the summer?"

"I'm an islander. I'm at the hotel all year."

"What do you think about a casino up-island?"

"I hate it."

Mathias took back his five dollars, crumpled it in his huge hand, and dropped it on the bar.

CHAPTER 7
I LOVE FUNERALS

THE FUNERAL OF NORA WINNETUKQET was sparsely attended. The Middletown Cemetery off State Road in West Tisbury wasn't easy to find unless you knew to look for the big tree as your point of navigation. Among the tall grass and rosehip bushes, Nora was getting ready to make her bed with other Winnetukqets who were century-old neighbors to the Mayhews, the Daggetts, the Coffins. New Englanders measured their tenure in centuries, and if you hadn't arrived on the island with Gosnold or lived there as a whale-hunting Indian, you were never as good as those who had.

Ray opened the passenger door of the white Volvo for his mother, her jeweled hand gripping him for support. Anne, never one to give up an audience, wore white sandals, wide-legged black trousers, a zebra-striped silk blouse, dark sunglasses, and a two-foot-wide straw hat to keep her porcelain skin unblemished. Strutting like an aged movie star, she put one hand on her son's arm, the other on the top of her head to hold down her hat. For the better part of that morning, Ray could hear his mother talking to herself, considering pearls versus diamonds, how hot it would be and how long she would have to stand in the hot sun with no place to sit and if any of the people she knew that Nora knew would be there and hoped they showed up looking like decent people and not like they were working on a farm. Ray knew his mother would out-glamour everyone else there. He never doubted that anywhere she went, especially to a funeral. Anne could do a funeral like no one else.

"You think they could have put some chairs out, it's so damn hot," Anne complained.

A priest in black with a white collar held the attention of about a dozen people, half of them neighbors curious about the mysterious end to a recluse. Anne surveyed the crowd. One woman brought flowers, but most looked like they stopped in on their way to farming the fields or dog grooming.

"Nobody around here knows how to dress. You think they could find a decent thing to put on for a dead woman. If you come to my funeral dressed like that I'll never forgive you,."

"You know who paid for this scraggly party? Ammons."

"You're kidding."

"Technically they never divorced, so it looks good for him if he does the right thing. But he doesn't get a dime of her money. I checked and the house and all her property she left to the—get this—MV animal shelter."

"You know, she had a dog, and it was hit by a car one summer and it was like the world was coming to an end. Well, every dog has his day, right?" Anne laughed.

"He's here."

In a neat dark suit and no tie, Henry Ammons walked slowly toward the congregation, holding a small bouquet. He came alone. He walked past Anne and Ray could sense she was getting ready to let one loose.

"That was a very nice thing you did…for your wife."

Henry stopped mid step and turned to Anne who was smiling broadly, waving now. Ray pulled her hand down.

"Ma, give it a break," Ray hushed.

Anne continued, nearly shouting, "If she didn't leave you anything, so what. You're the better person for what you did for her."

"I said shut it."

Henry walked on. He stopped next to the casket and placed the flowers on top.

Ray leaned in to his mother to continue the story and hopefully keep her from talking.

"Jerry said the governor's office wanted closure. Ammons is her closest living relative so, naturally, he steps up and takes care of it. Out of his own pocket."

"What about the people that did this to her? When are you going to catch them?"

Ray grimaced.

"We're working on it."

Anne opened her enormous pocketbook and took out an oversized piece of mail and waved it like a fan.

"Nora was a difficult woman, but no one deserves to be killed like that. What did she ever do to anyone?"

The priest, done with his last prayers, sprinkled holy water on the casket and closed his Bible. Some people shook hands before parting, but most just walked away in silence. Henry lingered a bit, long enough for Anne to approach him.

"You know, I used to see your wife around. What a nice woman, everyone said such nice things about her."

Henry kept his eyes on the casket. "That's nice of you to say so. I don't understand this at all. Nora kept to herself. She didn't care what people thought, she only cared about what she believed was right. I wish I could have helped her more."

"Don't be so hard on yourself. I'm sure you were good to her," Anne put her hand on Henry's arm.

"That's what everyone is telling me." He stuck out his hand. "Henry. Nice to meet you both."

"Ray. This is my mother, Anne."

"You work at the Tisbury police, right?" asked Henry.

"Sort of. I'm assisting with your wife's case."

"Oh, well, I don't know what I can tell you. Nora and I met years ago at a rally in Boston. We were together for a while and then I went into politics and she couldn't stomach it. She said I lost my principles."

"Ray, you should be in politics. You should be running for something." Anne was still fanning herself with half off turkey breast. "What do you do, Mr. Ammons?"

"I work in the governor's office."

"*Ooooh*." Anne widened her mouth, nodded approvingly. "I hope for your sake he wins. They look good so it makes it easier to win. My husband used to say you have to be good-looking to be in politics. And dress nice. None of this going-casual stuff…people dressing like slobs. The governor's wife, whatshername, she looks good. Always dressed up."

Ray held his tongue, a quiet escort, and let his mother chase whatever butterfly she was going after.

Anne continued helpfully, "I saw her picture in the paper, in a nice summer dress, and with that gorgeous ring. That must be worth a fortune. You know, my husband and I were in the jewelry business so I know. You'd have to chop off my hand before I took off a ring like that."

Henry stood there, Anne's hand still on his arm, and peered into her dark sunglasses. Ray was also staring at her. The butterfly landed on a stick of dynamite.

"That's right, if you want to be in politics, you gotta look good," she continued, "because people want to think good things about you. No matter what's really going on, keep your chin up and don't complain."

"Sounds like you should run for something, Anne."

"Of course I should! I was president of the women's auxiliary."

The first few minutes Ray and Anne were back in the car, they didn't speak. Ray was deep in thought about two new women in his life—Nora and Donna. Anne dug through her purse for a stick of gum, unwrapped it, and smacked it around loudly.

"Really?" Ray complained. "You can't stand people around here dressing like slobs and you chew gum like a mule."

"You know what I don't understand?" Anne wasn't listening. "Why would a good-looking guy like that Henry not have a girlfriend? He's in politics. He knows people. His wife left him a long time ago. That don't make sense."

"Maybe he does."

"Then where is she? What kind of woman doesn't go to a funeral with you?"

"Maybe she's…" Ray's brain came alive with a half-baked idea. He pulled over the car.

"What the hell…?"

"Just be quiet. I'm going to tell you something that only the police know, and I'm only telling you because I think you're on to something. When Jerry and I did a sweep at Nora's house that night, we found Donna's engagement ring. It was upstairs on the bathroom floor."

"On the floor? Why the hell didn't you tell me?"

"What if Henry Ammons and Donna McKenna are seeing each other? She's been feigning heat strokes and asking to be dropped off in strange places. What if Nora's house was a meeting point for them?" Ray paused and sank down into the seat. The half-baked story felt almost right.

"I could believe it. Why not? She probably hates her husband, and this guy is around, and it's her way to stick it to him. What's her husband gonna do, leave her? Not if he's running for reelection. She'd have to fall off a boat drunk first."

"Why Nora's house? Did she agree to let them meet because she got something out of it? Did they go to see her about something? The three don't mix, but the thread is Ammons."

Ray turned the car back onto the road.

"Stop at Cronig's and get me some rub-offs." Anne took twenty dollars out of her enormous purse and smacked her gum.

Donna sat up in the hospital bed and reached for her phone, buried deep inside a Burberry purse. She used Siri to call "Madam LaRoux," her fifteen-dollar-per-minute confidant, soothsayer, love counselor, medium to the outer worlds. If there was one person Donna felt at ease with, it was the mothering Madam, patient and kind as the minutes ticked ticked ticked.

Madam LaRoux picked up, enunciating each syllable. "Hallooow, Donna?"

"Madam, oh thank God, I need to talk to you. Philip brought me to the hospital but he's gone, of course. I don't know where he went, again. I'm afraid to call Henry… and I lost my engagement ring. I'm totally alone. No one will help me."

"Caaaaaalm yourself, child. I hear great pain in your heart, yes, I hear pain. I can feeeeeel it. You are betrayed not once, but now twice. Your lover who was once your comfort is now distant."

"Why isn't he here?"

Sobs. Heaving sobs because she was alone, sick, and angry. Most of all, she felt used up and left to rot, a browning apple softening into the earth. Time was taking her good looks, her body, her better opportunities with someone else. The hourglass of youth was at the end.

"Your lover…yes, he wants to come to you but—I see he is conflicted. There is a great pain in his heart because of his love for you."

"When will he come? I need him here now."

"You must be strong, my child. Let him come to you, like a moth to the flame. He has desire for you, but he is conflicted. When he is ready, he will come."

"Is he scared of Philip? My husband?"

"I see a man…and a woman."

"It is his ex-wife? She just passed away. She knew about me and Henry because—well, we met at her house a few times when we knew she was away. It was stupid. Completely stupid. But we were desperate to see each other, and we knew that no one would think we were there. And she found out, and we begged her not to say anything…"

"Love makes us impulsive, my child."

"She knew Henry worked for my husband. She threatened us, saying she would tell my husband, and Henry would lose his job unless he did something for her. And Philip and I would divorce and I'd be God knows where without a husband or anyone to take care of me. And now…she's dead."

"Yeeeesss, yes, yes." Madam LaRoux's voice climbed. "You have angered her spirit. She will not be at peace until she gets what she wants."

The medium started to sing, a low, chanting hum that went on for minutes. Donna lay still, her face buried in the bed sheets, until it was over.

"I need to find my ring. I need Henry to come get me."

"Dear child, find the strength within and you will find all your heart desires."

Donna thanked her and hung up the phone. Her body was exhausted from crying, her muscles shook from withdrawal of the narcotics. Digging in her purse again she found a compact mirror and popped it open, horrified at what she saw. Her eyes were bloodshot. The creases around her mouth made deep marionette lines. Her skin was raw and sallow. She clicked the compact closed and turned her face into the pillow, like turning into her grave.

Softly, the door to her hospital room opened. Philip stood with his hand on the handle, the other holding a huge bouquet of white roses—her wedding flower. He stood and looked at her for a few seconds, then took a seat on her bed and touched her side. She sat up, startled, but his gesture was calming.

"Donna…"

She burst out crying and fell onto his shoulder. Hard, heaving sobs shook her. Philip smoothed her hair like petting a dog.

"Shhhh. It's okay, baby. I'm here. I need you to stick with me, okay? We're a team, right?"

"Philip…I lost my ring." She got the words out between choking sobs. Priorities.

"I know, baby. We're gonna get it back."

CHAPTER 8
PEOPLE ARE NOT THAT COMPLICATED

"THE CASE IS STUCK." RAY rubbed his hair and pushed aside his dish. "No one is making any progress. Busick least of all."

Anne pushed the leftover dinner out of the way, reached across the kitchen table and took out a deck of playing cards from a case carved with the knave of hearts. She set up the deck for solitaire, seven across, six face down. Ray knew this is how it needed to start for Anne. Solitaire put the crazy world under the microscope of her kitchen lamp. Turning each card over and making little piles, cheating when needed, so long as it kept the game moving along. As she played she looked up to the ceiling as if to call on the ghost of Christmases past.

"All right, Ray. Let's go way back. When God put man in the world. What did people do back then? They hunted, right? They killed each other. They made babies. You gotta think, Ray, nothing is any different than it used to be. You gotta go back to the beginning and think about people's *brains*. Think about what they really want. They want love. Revenge. They wanna feel secure. You know, I watched fifteen seasons of Forensic Files. People are not that complicated."

Anne shuffled the cards in her hand and shook her head. She was already losing this hand but kept going.

"Be logical. Why would someone kill a woman who hardly left her house and gave her money to the pet shelter? Did she anger someone? Did someone think she was rich? Did she find out something she shouldn't have?"

"All right, so let's think about it your way." Ray was irritated. "Nora isn't insanely rich, no one is madly in love with her, and she's not in love with anyone that we can turn up. So whadda we got?"

"Exactly. Nothing fits. Except…" Anne leaned forward and pointed her finger, "that she knew *something*."

"All right, what did she know?"

Anne slapped the table.

"That's what you gotta find out. What did she know up there in the woods. Who came to visit her? What kind of people did she see?"

Anne was throwing her head back and rocking in her kitchen chair.

"Yup, someone came to see her, and she found out something, and they found out something about her, and that's why she had to go." Anne shuffled the cards again, then scooped them up in her hands to start the game over.

"I'm going to bed. This isn't going anywhere."

And when Ray climbed into his garage apartment, with cold sheets and the full-faced moon in the window bending its light in on him, he had the itch that she was right. Nora knew something. In his mind he laid the players out on the table, his mental game of solitare, starting with Henry Ammons, her estranged husband working for the governor who was summering on the island. He knew somehow Donna McKenna's engagement ring wound up on Nora's bathroom floor. How did the ring get there if Nora didn't steal it? And it wasn't a payoff because Nora didn't need money. Therefore, Donna by herself or with Henry must have been in that house to talk to Nora. For what reason?

Suddenly Ray shot from his bed and back into Anne's kitchen.

"Ma! You said you sometimes talked to Nora, and you said she was against the casino that's being built in Aquinnah?"

Anne was washing dishes with yellow rubber gloves. She didn't bother to turn around.

"Ooooh, yeah. She wasn't gonna go for some big-city nonsense in her neck of the woods. I think she tried to, you know, organize. Get people to shut it down."

"Did she tell you this directly? That she was organizing an effort to block it?"

"Every chance she got. Wouldn't stop talking about it."

"Did she say exactly what she was planning on doing?"

Anne turned around. She put her hand on her hip.

"You know, she didn't, but she said she knew someone who could block the whole thing. You know, big-shot kinda person."

"It must have been Ammons. Who else would she know with that kind of power? Like you said, who did she know up there in the woods?"

"And he could put the bug in the ear of the governor…"

"And if Ammons was having an affair with the governor's wife and Nora knew about it…"

"That's just enough reason to get your ex-husband to listen to you."

"So, let's draw this one step further. Nora says to Ammons, you stop this casino or I'm going to let the governor know about you and his wife."

"Probably." Anne nodded her head.

"And Ammons…kills her to shut her up? No. Too far-fetched." Ray knew Ammons would be exposed and lose his job, but it wasn't worth life in prison. Donna would be caught up in it too, but something told Ray she would land on her feet.

Ray continued, "But let's say Nora threatens Ammons, tells him to shut it down. Maybe they meet. Henry goes to see Nora. He promises her that he'll talk the governor out of it so she'll shut up about the affair."

"Promises he can't keep."

"So he sits on it. Doesn't say anything to the governor…and then what? Gets lucky that someone else bumps her off? So who else wants her gone?"

"The people behind the casino for one. But is that enough for murder? We're talking about a junky bingo hall!"

"The reality is, Ma, she's dead. And someone around her did it. Like you said, it wasn't for money because no one got any. But there is a benefit to her shutting up. Henry, Donna McKenna want her quiet. Mathias and all the Wampanoags that want the casino want her quiet so they can string up a lynching rope. You know, white man's noose and all that. One of them could have thought she was a real threat. Maybe someone saw her talking to Ammons…" Ray's voice trailed off. There was some thread there to pull on.

"I told you she knew something! I told you! I was right."

"Yes, Ma. You're always right."

And Ray kissed his mother on the cheek, giving her the pleasure of the winning hand, and she went back to washing dishes.

CHAPTER 9
FIRES

ATHIAS WAITED OUTSIDE THE GAY Head Community Center in his truck. He'd just hung up with the treasurer of the Wampanoag tribe of Mashpee. A wire for three hundred thousand dollars was coming directly to his account at Edgartown Savings Bank tomorrow, just in time to pay the workers to keep going, and, more importantly, for the slot machines.

The slots were coming tonight, on the last freight ferry, from Global Entertainment of Oklahoma City. The company had called ahead, making sure the address was right, that it was an island the machines were going to, and there was a boat involved. Mathias had laughed into the phone, "It's easy. The driver just sits in the vehicle. Nothing to worry about."

Mathias rubbed his hands excitedly. This was the progress he wanted. With funds from Mashpee, he could buy a few high-power generators, the slots could go in, and he could open the doors in a few weeks and catch the month of August. He closed his eyes, imagining that opening weekend, and leaned back against the headrest, breathing contently. With tribal funds, the vote of the Wampanoag council, and the governor staying out of his business, Mathias could play a winning hand. Screw the town permits. He was here first. Thirteen thousand years first.

His phone rang again. With a laugh in his voice, he answered. "Yeah. Yes. Who's this?"

"This is your delivery from Global Entertainment. I got sixteen machines for a Mathias Winnepeg."

"Hah, that's me."

"I need you to send a repair guy. I got two flats."

"What do you mean?"

"Someone flatted me. Some assholes flatted my tires while I set up in the cabin. I can't get off this goddamn boat."

"Okay. Okay. I'll send someone down there." He hung up, still exuberant.

Mathias called a few of his Brazilians and sent them down to fix the flats, get the truck off the ferry, and get the slots up to the center. The men loaded the machines off the truck in the darkness, no words. It felt covert and thrilling to watch them load in, each machine sizzled in the moonlight with the anticipation of a big score. Mathias locked the building for the first time in weeks and went home for the best sleep of his life.

Hours later, at three in the morning, a wailing of sirens woke him. It was an unusual time for emergency vehicles, even in the crush of the summer season. The sirens crescendoed and dropped, a ceaseless circularity of rising and falling wails out of synch, never stopping. Were they coming closer or fading, Mathias couldn't tell. It was a swirl of ear-splitting cries. Then a glow crept into his windows, a dull glow of deep red that saturated his room.

His phone buzzed. A pang hit his stomach. He answered. A scared voice said he needed to come immediately, that the community center was on fire, that everyone was afraid it might spread to their houses, and what was Mathias going to do to save the reservation and all they had worked for.

Wearing only shorts, Mathias flew from his house into his truck and floored it.

It can't be. I was just there.

The road up to the community center parking lot was jammed with fire trucks, police cars, and ambulances, so he four-wheeled it between houses, the truck chewing through front and back yards. He came as close as he could before being blocked by more vehicles, then sprang out his truck with a mouthful of curses and walked closer to the fire, holding up his hands to shield his face from the scorching heat. Mathias stood paralyzed in a time-bending vortex of disbelief and sensory overload, processing everything he saw as a nightmare he would wake from any second. But it went on and on. The Gay Head Community Center was a wooden pyramid engulfed—hellish, five-story flames burst out, snapping and ripping the air with orange-black smoke and fire hot as an open oven. In the oven burned the soul of Mathias: the years of arduous planning, the years of selling out to politicians, the promises made to his tribe, the promises made to himself.

"Stand back!"

A fireman in an oxygen mask motioned for him to move back. Mathias didn't move, never taking his eyes away. A cop came up and grabbed his arm.

"Winnetukqet, you gotta leave. It's too dangerous."

No response.

"You need to move back," the officer shouted.

"Who the fuck did this?!" Mathias screamed at the inferno. "I'll kill him!"

"Mathias…we think it's a gas leak…an accident. We got the call twenty minutes ago and got here as fast as we could. That's all we know. You gotta move," he pleaded.

"Someone did this. You hear me? Someone wants me to murder them…"

The community center burned all night despite three towns sending everything they had to stop it. Mathias watched until dawn broke, then left without saying another word.

The next morning was a gorgeous summer day, and the sun shone on charred piles of wood and black water. Birds landed and pecked at the wood, squirrels ran over it like fallen trees in the forest. Only the heap of melted slot machines looked out of place, warped, and dead on arrival.

By seven a.m. the news of the fire was out on both the *Gazette* and *Vineyard Times* websites, had also been picked up by *Reuters*, *AP*, *The Boston Globe*, *The New York Times*, and *NBC4*, with links pointing back to the tiny Vineyard servers gasping for bandwidth. Ray had only his phone, the signal over the local cell towers coming in at a drip's pace, sputtering an already excruciatingly slow load time. But finally he saw them: a gallery of pictures of the fire, the small reservation overrun with emergency vehicles, the charred skeleton of its once-promising community center, and to everyone's near universal surprise, the melted slot machines with triple cherries and golden treasure chests still visible on the wheels. The articles paid just about lip service to the fire followed by paragraphs of hyperbolic consternation as to how the hell these machines of evil and sin could have sneaked in with no one watching. The online editorial sections were aghast with fire and brimstone, hell and highwater, for the machines that dared infiltrate the sanctity of island life. What trash. What vandalism. On the other side of the circus tent, the fair-share capitalists took shots at the snobbery of those "not in my backyard" people that "denied others the right to make a living." It was a full-on mudslinging that gave the publications the best, and worst, day of their existence.

Ray's phone buzzed. It was Jerry.

"I have you on the clock today starting at nine, which is the start time of the governor's press conference."

"What press conference? Where?"

"At the fire scene. It's going to be a wicked day and I need everyone I can get. If you get to the station in the next fifteen, we can ride up. Otherwise, you need to drive yourself."

"I'm there. Just gotta drop off some stuff for my mother."

Ray trotted up to the porch and dropped twenty dollars in scratch-off tickets on the table. His mother was nowhere in sight.

"Ma! I gotta go *right* now. We're going up to the fire scene in Gay Head. The one that happened last night that I told you about. The governor is giving a press conference."

His mother leaned out of the bathroom in curlers. "You just tell me if his wife shows up."

———————————

Governor McKenna stepped from a polished black Escalade and walked through the sooty parking lot of the community center to assess the scene. Spilling out behind him were Busick, Ammons, a few aides, and several reporters. The crew set up lights and a makeshift press conference area with plenty of charred remains to fill the shot. Every Wampanoag from the reservation was already there, waiting, plus residents who walked miles once the news spread of the presser. Phones were held high to record whatever was about to happen.

"I want to thank everyone for coming out this morning, on what otherwise would be a gorgeous summer day, to once again confront a tragedy," started the governor. "Behind me is the burned-out remains of a spot of great significance to the Wampanoag tribe of Aquinnah. This community center was a place for cultural celebration, for preserving a great heritage that is part of the fabric of this island."

There wasn't a sound from the hundreds standing. A screeching murder of crows signaled the end was nigh.

"As a longtime supporter of the Wampanoag tribe, I'm here to stand with you, to help you rebuild, and give you whatever resources are needed. The state of

Massachusetts will act and preserve a critical part of its heritage."

Governor McKenna motioned, and Mathias stepped forward.

"Mathias Winnetukqet is the elected tribal leader of the Wampanoags of Aquinnah. Many of you know him as an inspiration and a friend to all. I give you my word that I am here to support you in whatever way needed to bring back the sense of community that was lost here last night."

The governor placed his hand on Mathias's shoulder and let him step center stage.

"Thank you, Governor. I am more than heartbroken, I am angry. I still cannot believe this has happened. I will not let it stop our plans from moving forward. The tribe will rebuild, and this time we will have the full support of the governor's office to get us the permits we need, to rebuild bigger, better. We will bring the tribe the life-supporting revenue it needs just like every other tribe in the state has been permitted to do. We have been fighting for years against oppressive rules. We do not believe in these rules. The Wampanoags are a warrior tribe. We have fought for our lands for thousands of years. We will keep fighting this injustice…"

The governor cut him off.

"To that end, Lieutenant Busick of the Boston PD is here supporting my office to ensure we take swift action and that there is no further danger to the Wampanoag community or anyone else. Now we'll take a few questions."

Every eye locked on Busick. The dam broke.

"Is there any connection between the fire and the death of Nora Winnetukqet? The deccased was a known member of the Wampanoag tribe."

"No. Next."

"Is there any connection with the murder of Winnetukqet and the report of another Indian male found by the Coast Guard a few days later? What's the status—"

"No. We are treating it as an unrelated accident. Next."

"But the report is that he may have been from the same tribe. And you're saying there's no connection?"

The reporter's jab made Busick out as stupid, questioning his top-crime-avenger status.

"I'll repeat, we have no evidence to connect the two. Next question."

"Andy Bachelor, *MV Times*. County records show that Ms. Winnetukqet was married to Henry Ammons, the governor's campaign manager. Is Ammons being treated as a suspect?"

Before Busick could respond, the governor nudged him off the podium.

"This has been a great shock for Henry, who I consider a friend and close colleague. At this time, Henry is not a suspect, and I hope that you will give him a chance to grieve a person he once loved."

"*MV Gazette*. Governor, did you consider closing the airport and ferries?"

"It was a difficult decision, but the airport and ferries are covered in cameras. If our suspect tried to leave, we'll know it."

"So you *have* a suspect?"

"No comment."

"A follow-up question, Governor. Slot machines were found in the rubble behind you. Were these here with permission of the state?"

"The tribe, as you know, is in the midst of a back-and-forth regarding the interpretation of a federal rite that allows for a Class II gaming facility. The state has no jurisdiction in deciding federal matters."

"Sir, did you know the slot machines were here?"

"No."

The governor lingered on the podium for a few more questions, but Ray had heard enough to know they were bluffing their way through the press conference and were no closer to solving Nora's murder than he was.

From the corner of his eye, Ray saw Jerry walking toward a familiar truck with a Tasmanian Devil sticker. Andrew Cogswell reclined in the driver's seat, windows down, drinking a beer. It wasn't the first of the morning, either, from the looks of it. He downed it, crushed the can in his fist, reached for another.

"Looks like a Redskins party, Jer. Are they playing the Pats?"

"Did you hear about this gas leak?"

"I always smell 'em first." Cogswell guffawed and slapped the dash. "Besides, I didn't think these tepees could get a gas line."

"Look, Drew, get out of your vehicle and walk yourself home. I don't want to write you up."

"All rightyyy, Officer Friendly…" And rolling out of his truck, saluted Jerry like a drunken sailor and stumbled toward the main road.

Hours later, Andrew was dead to the world, snoring loudly on his couch. He tripped across the ledge of his back door, leaving it wide open, crawled through the galley kitchen floor to the living room, and planted his face in the couch cushions. The alcohol pumping through his body flooded his brain with contorted, erotic thoughts.

He was dreaming of her, of Nora. In his dream her body was engulfed in the flames of the burning building. Her long white arms stretched out to him as she floated above the ground, wearing a loose dress that disintegrated in the fire, the air turning red with flame and black with smoke. Then she was standing on the rock, the rock of Moshup, birds pecking her naked flesh until it spurted blood like raindrops. Her eyes were gone, eaten by the birds, and yet her face, covered in sand, looked peaceful.

Andrew threw rocks at the seagulls until one dove for him. That startled him awake.

Rolling over, he hugged the cushion. He had never dreamed of Nora before. He'd met her at the pet shelter when he brought in a stray cat with an eye hanging out of its socket, and Nora didn't flinch. She wrapped its face in a towel and thanked him for doing what he could. Andrew hadn't found her sexy—she was coarse as horse hair and flat as a baseball field. But she had a kindness at the edges. After that, he brought her stray dogs and busted birds, making whatever conversation he could each time, feeling a small pang in his chest when she stood close.

Then there was the day Nora's dog was hit by an SUV and she brought it to the ER. The driver either didn't notice or didn't bother to stop. Nora was in pieces. She called him, and he took her out and got her drunk. She cried while they had sex in the back of his truck like teenagers. Slowly, they both opened the creaky doors to their soft, vulnerable spots and found more in common than a need to help unlucky animals. They despised golf courses, mega yachts, shark tournaments, and mostly, the casino.

"I'll never understand him," Nora had said. "I hate that we are the same blood."

"Who?"

"Mathias. We're somehow cousins when you draw a line down from his grandparents. He's only doing this casino because he's a broken person. I want to feel sorry for him, but I can't. When I see him I tell him I'm disgusted to be related to him. And I'm sickened by how he uses the tribe and manipulates them."

"The casino is not going to happen. He doesn't have the approvals to do it. I won't approve it."

"Drew, it doesn't matter to him. No one matters to Mathias except Mathias. That's just the person he is. No one gets through to him. He's like ice."

"The town is not going to approve his shitty bingo hall. He'd have to kill me first."

Drew rolled over again, trying to get back to his dream. He needed to kill the birds, get her off the rock, wrap her in a blanket. His brain swam in alcohol and his blood in hormones, pounding, pounding. The pounding got louder and harder. It was coming up from the floor. *Someone is trying to jackhammer through my floor*. He raised his hand and covered his face. The hammering got to his temples like icepicks. His face was wet, bloated, hot. If only the pounding would stop, he could go back to dreaming of her.

"Drew. Wake up."

"Uuuuhhhhhh."

"Come on. Get up."

Two hands grabbed his arms and lifted his limp body to a sitting position. He fell to the floor. The hands tried again and got him back on the couch, this time with his head thrown back, his mouth wide open.

"Uuuuhhhhhh. Go away."

"Drew, I've got a warrant for your arrest."

"Fuuuuuuuckuuuuuu."

"Andrew Cogswell, man, I hate to do this, but I'm arresting you on suspicion of arson. Anything you say…"

"Gofuckyerseeeeef." He flopped on his face.

Drew was again lifted and dragged across the floor, limp as a two-hundred-pound carcass, outside into the blaring noonday sun. He was dumped into the back of a police cruiser. Jerry was at the wheel. Drew pulled himself up, nearly threw up, and swallowed the acid back down.

"Whaddayawant, Jer?"

Jerry leaned over the front bench seat, sighed.

"Look, Drew, if you did it, I understand."

"Did what?"

"Drew, we know you've been against the casino from the start. That day at the tribe meeting you made sure everyone knew. And now we've got someone from the reservation who saw your truck nearby an hour before the fire started. Were you there?"

"That cocksucker got what he deserved. Booooom!"

Jerry turned around and shook his head. His to-do list wasn't getting any shorter.

Andrew Cogswell, stinking drunk and smug, was booked at three-thirty that afternoon in the Edgartown jail. He had nothing else to say except to ask for six aspirin and a bottle of water. He didn't want a phone call or a lawyer.

The jail cell was an old hotel room with a cot, one window, no shade. Drew stared at the ceiling, waiting for the aspirin to kick in and calm the pounding in his skull. After a few minutes, he walked to the wall and mashed the button on the intercom.

"I want out of this shit hole. Open this door."

"If you're ready, Drew, we're ready for you."

Drew was brought to an interview room that used to be a butler's pantry. It was a cozy set up for Jerry, Drew, and the other officer minding the recording equipment. Someone had taped a sign, "SMILE, you're being recorded!" to the wall. Drew laughed at how Podunk friendly the island's jail was.

"Interview commencing at five-thirty p.m...."

"Drew, let's not make this hard. We'll give you all the breaks if you just tell us…"

Drew snorted, sucked the phlegm through his sinuses, and cut him off.

"The only thing you need to know…I'm guessin' you know about the in'jin the Coast Guard hauled in about a week ago? I was there. I saw it on the deck of *JAD*."

"What about it?"

"The chief did it. Nailed that guy."

"Chief who?"

"Winnetukqet, dumbass. The chief nailed him 'cause he was going to change his vote for building the casino.

Ask for a new vote. Chiefy doesn't like that. He wants his little in'jins to stay in line. I know what's going on. The chief thinks I'm stupid like the rest of you, but I know what's going on. Like the night he brought the slot machines on a freighter, thinking no one was watching. I got eyes everywhere. I know every goddamn thing that goes on on this island. Steamship. CG. I'm standing up for the spineless islanders. Committees and lawyers don't do shit…drag on for years while the chief's got those Brazilians on the clock…with *my* tax dollars."

"Drew, did you cut the gas line and start the fire at the Gay Head Community Center?"

"If I did, I did you weak sons-of-bitches a favor. I need a beer." Andrew rubbed his face and leaned back in his chair.

The other officer spoke up, "How do you know Winnetukqet is responsible for the death of the John Doe found by the fishing vessel?"

"Drop the charges and I'll tell you."

There was a knock on the door. Jerry was asked to step out of the interview room for an urgent call. He went into a closet-sized room, put the phone on mute plus speaker, leaned against the wall, and felt the onslaught of Busick's Boston spittle.

"How the hell can things be getting worse and we still have no leads? The governor's patience is running out. Do you think this is the only case I'm working?"

Jerry was silent. He was too tired to fight with big-city Busick. Jerry just wanted to be a good cop, help tourists find their hotels, be the assistant coach of the high school football team. Over the years, the summers had become increasingly trying, and this summer was hands down the worst in island history. The local economy had lost an incalculable amount of money from tourists choosing to go other places where there weren't fires and dead Indians ruining their good time. Jerry's team at the Tisbury police station looked like Mayberry clowns with bulging eyes, way out of their league.

Busick's dressing down wasn't going to get anything done. It was checking a box labeled "Called Tisbury, passed the blame, took any credit there was to get." After a few minutes of ear gnawing, he got to a question.

"Is there any connection with the murder and the fire at the bingo hall?"

"Maybe."

"What's 'maybe'?"

"We arrested a man today. We have eyewitnesses placing his vehicle there at the time the gas line was supposedly cut, which is likely the source of the fire."

"What's the motive? Disgruntled village person?"

"Something like that. Local mercenary who thinks he's saving the town from depravity."

"Is he also a suspect for the murders?"

"No, but he says if we drop the arson charge, he's going to prove Mathias Winnetukqet is responsible for the other man found by the Coast Guard."

Busick breathed into the phone like a bull before killing the matador. "I want to talk to this guy."

Henry Ammons was on a three-way conference call. Dialed in from tribal headquarters in Mashpee was the chief of the New England Wampanoag tribe, Amos "Little Drum" Ousamequin, along with the governor. Little Drum was making a big noise on what Henry thought was a small matter regarding Nora's funeral, which he had arranged and paid for. Nora's American Indian heritage entitled her to a tribal ceremony, and some guy in a black cassock was not Amos's idea of dust in the wind.

"I'm surprised that we were not told immediately. We would have arranged for her body to be brought to Mashpee and given full rites."

"Amos, she had no immediate next of kin. She was also recently autopsied, and we needed to put the matter to rest."

"That's another thing I'm not pleased to hear. We should have received notice before the autopsy. We know it's not law here like other states, but the spirit has a right not to suffer needlessly."

"This is a murder investigation. I would hope there's no objection."

The governor, who had been silent up until that point, broke the scuffle.

"My apologies if things were mishandled, Amos. This is an unprecedented situation for many reasons, and my team is using their best judgment."

"Is there any connection with Nora Winnetukqet and the fire at Gay Head? I feel there is so much hate right now. Everyone I talk to is scared to raise their voice. We have a right to make a living. It's part of the federal law."

"Exactly, Amos. And in light of the circumstances around Nora's death and the fire, even if they're unrelated, I think it's better to postpone any movement on the Gay Head development. As you said, too much hate, and it's small dollars, anyway, compared to the other projects we're planning."

Amos took a long pause. A cheap office chair creaked through the receiver. Henry held his breath and knew the next one to speak would lose the negotiation.

"This will kill Mathias," said Amos.

"I think we can all agree it's better this way."

"What's the message?"

"To start, we know many locals are against gaming. We've been trying the delicate balance and will continue, etc. But we quietly let this die, look like good sports and let sympathy smooth the rails in other zones. Henry can work up the release."

"I'll get on that, governor."

McKenna continued, "We're losing a few thousand square feet, maybe a few hundred thousand a year from Gay Head, but what's the same square footage applied to the Two Feathers project in Barnstable? Probably five or six times the return."

Amos's voice smiled through the phone. Instead of a creaking chair, a cash register was ringing.

"Now I see what governors do."

CHAPTER 10
THE FINGER

RACHEL WAS MORE GORGEOUS THAN ever that afternoon in her tiny black bikini, skin glowing in the sunshine, tan lines suggestive of hours spent lying on the beach. She hadn't eaten anything substantial since Friday afternoon, when Dennis locked up the office and went back to Maine for the weekend to see his wife, three kids, and dying father-in-law. Rachel stared out at the ocean, replaying over and over the way Dennis kissed her before going to the ferry, whispering, *"I'll be back soon, baby. Don't let that fire go out while I'm gone."*

Rachel had been dating older men since she was nineteen, and knew enough of the world to know she had Dennis hooked. She was the ocean breeze in his diurnal monotony of adulthood. And yet, he got on the ferry and left her. Left her with the traces of his wet kisses all over her body, the sound of his words over and over until she started to hate herself. She had to stop. She knew she could have any guy on the beach. If only she wanted a single one of them. Rachel treated men with the coolness of a cat that sleeps where it wants, goes out when it feels like it, and comes back when it's hungry. Except for Dennis.

On the beach, she recognized a few people, said hi. One was the lifeguard, Matt, with his floppy hair and Ray Bans, the quintessential lifeguard body—very tan, very fit. He was easy enough to look at when there was a gaping knife wound in Rachel's ego.

"Hey, Rach."

"Hey."

"You coming to Squibby tonight? We're getting some people together."

"Maybe. Depends."

"Hey, want to hear something crazy?"

"Okay."

"I was doing beach cleanup, and I found a finger."

"You did not."

"Shit you not. It had a ragged end, like it was eaten off by sharks."

Rachel laughed. "If you think that's so impressive, I saw the dead guy it came from. *All* of his flesh had been eaten off by sharks."

"How did you see it?"

"I work at the hospital a few days a week."

"Smarty pants."

"If you find any more body parts, you should let the police know. They came down to see the body. Apparently, no one knows who it is."

"You wanna see it? The finger?"

"I do."

Rachel reached out her hand and let Matt pull her up from her beach towel. He led her to the guard house, where he had put the finger in a plastic bag and then in the communal refrigerator. Living up to Ray's prediction, Rachel would have made a good cop. She called the Tisbury police and reported the finger found on the beach, then handed the phone to Matt and made him give all the details.

Officer Sawyer would soon be on his way to collect the digit, and the police told them to keep it in the bag in the fridge. Rachel walked out of the guard house unimpressed and validated that younger men were a waste of time.

The finger had enough print left on it for the police to match it to one Asa White, busted on a minor drug possession charge several years earlier. Asa had lived on the Aquinnah reservation with a roommate, and when Ray and Jerry knocked on the door a few hours later, there was no response. Looking in the window, Ray saw the place was dark, no cars.

They went over to the neighbor's and knocked. A dark, blank face opened the door just wide enough to show disdain.

"Sorry to bother you, miss," said Jerry. "We're the Tisbury police and we're looking for your neighbor, Asa White. Have you seen him recently?"

"No."

"Do you know the last time he was home?"

"I don't know. Maybe a while. You should ask Mathias."

Ray jumped in. "What would Mathias know?"

"Mathias just knows…everyone."

The woman now seemed scared, in a rush to close the door.

"Do you know where Asa worked? Any friends or family members we can talk to?" Jerry asked.

"No. I don't know him. He just lives there."

Jerry let out a long sigh. "We have reason to believe Asa may have drowned and are trying to establish when he was last seen or heard."

The woman didn't change her expression. "I don't know anything about that."

The door began to close, but Ray stuck out his hand to keep it open. "Did you know Nora Winnetukqet?"

In the woman's blank face, Ray noticed a flicker.

"No. Talk to Mathias, he knew her I think."

"All roads lead to Mathias, huh? Why is that?" Ray continued.

"He's the head of our tribe. He looks out for everyone. Gives my son jobs to stay out of trouble. I thought you came here to ask about my son, Jesse."

"Is your son in trouble? Anything we can help with?"

The woman closed her mouth firmly.

"How old is your son, Mrs…"

"Vanderhoop," she relinquished.

"Vanderhoop. How old is he? Is he about Asa's age? Maybe they know each other." Ray saw her face more than flickering now. She was mashing down her teeth and breathing harder, holding something behind her tongue, Ray sensed.

There was a noise behind her, coming from upstairs.

"Who is it?" the voice called down.

At the landing her son, Jesse, appeared, startled by the blue uniforms.

"We're looking for Asa," Ray called up. "Have you seen him?"

"I'm not talking to you, or anyone else. Get out of my house."

———————————

Ray and Jerry walked back to the car. The people in that house were scared of something, quick to dismiss Asa's death and quick to get rid of them. *All roads lead to Mathias*, Ray thought. Head of the tribe, protector of the little Indian. Keeps rowdy boys out of the pen. The bingo hall king. Able to get hundreds of thousands for slot machines and workers to install them.

Who or what was the source of Mathias's power? He obviously felt impervious to local roadblocks. So who was in his pocket? What did he know? Did someone have a vested stake in seeing this janky bingo joint hit the big time?

Maybe it was time to bring him in for questioning.

They got into the car, and Ray turned to Jerry, chief of police, elected protector of the islanders, little fish in a little pond. Ray had taken to Jerry, the way a father takes to an adopted son.

"Hey, Jer, I heard Cogswell just about admitted to the arson. Did he say why he did it?"

"Said it was a mercy crime because the legal process to stop Mathias was taking too long. If you ask me, I don't think Drew could stand Mathias going around him. I've known Drew a long time and, well, he's one big ego.

While Drew is telling me this in the Edgartown jail, your old boss Busick calls me for his daily status report and wants to talk to him."

"Busick? Drew's got nothing to do with Nora's death."

"Maybe. But he says Mathias killed the guy fished out of the sound. Of course, Drew's light on details, because in exchange for the proof he wants us to drop the arson charge."

"Two questions. Why would Mathias want to kill a fellow Indian? And that's a hell of a charge to drop for some information, even if it's true, isn't it?"

"To answer the first question, there's been infighting for decades, each side blaming the other for lack of progress or too much of it. Not worth killing over, but it could have gotten that far. Mathias has a rough past. His older brother was shot in front of him during a robbery. The family had a store on the mainland, someone broke in to rob it, and I think the guy got scared and the gun went off. Mathias is the youngest of eight kids. I think it scarred him forever seeing his oldest brother killed like that."

"When was this?"

"Oh, decades ago. Mathias was young, in his teens. Guy was high, asked for the cash in the register. Mathias's brother stepped in, and the guy freaked out and shot him. Terrible."

"So that's why he's got a frosty relationship with most people?"

"Could be. The guy who shot his brother was also the son of a big riverboat gambling owner. New America Cruises, or something like that. Ever been on a riverboat to gamble?"

"Jer, so what happened? Who's the guy and did he go to jail?"

"Oh man, you're asking me to go way back. I don't remember much more. I think the guy got a commuted sentence because he pleaded temporary insanity and had a good lawyer. Mathias's father, of course, was broken. He died a few years later from health issues. He was never the same after that."

Ray chewed his lip as he let it all marinate. That explained Mathias's to-hell-with-the-world attitude. Just a kid, sees his family screwed over by what money can buy, carries the incident around for a few decades until it turns his blood into piss. *Or maybe that's too easy a storyline,* he thought. Then Anne's words came into his head, as clearly as if she was in the back seat. *"People are not that complicated."*

"So, back to my second question. What makes Drew Cogswell think he's going to have these charges dropped in exchange for some information about Mathias and the dead guy?"

"Drew's a funny guy. Lives alone. I've known him for fifteen years and I couldn't tell you much except that he also worked at the gas station."

"I think it's time to talk to Mathias, Jer."

"That's his house right there," said Jerry with a timid smile. "You ready to meet the chief?"

Jerry and Ray turned onto a road called Moshup's Trail and then onto a long dirt driveway. Moss-covered stone walls lined both sides of the drive, and when the walls stopped, it opened to a wide, lush pasture. Beyond the pasture was a breath-taking view of the Atlantic Ocean, the kind of view you'd see in galleries and glossy real estate magazines: a panorama of sky, seabirds, and waves smoothing over the rocky beach with the clay cliffs in the distance. It was the natural world as it had been ten thousand years ago, before Gosnold and the whalers, before tourism, ice cream, and T-shirts. Nothing had touched this landscape except natural erosion and a few planks of wood to build Mathias's modest house set behind the dune.

Nailed to the exterior of the house were small and large animal skulls and bones—rabbits, deer, opossum, shark jaws, a whale tooth—blanched by salt and sun to a bright white. Bird feathers were knit into a giant dream catcher. A strange flute noise came from a bunch of reeds, catching the wind. Jerry and Ray could see Mathias, bent over on his knees, shirtless with his huge shoulders shaking and working, his hands clawing at the ground. He was gardening. The trim bed around his house had wild-looking but useful plants—milkweed, chamomile, Indian tobacco, and foxglove from what Ray could see. Ray couldn't keep a cactus alive in his apartment, but he had earned the Boy Scouts' plants-you-can-eat badge when he was twelve.

Mathias stood, turned around. At six-four, sweaty, and with hands like bear claws, he was not someone you'd want to meet in a dark alley, or in broad daylight. Ray thought of the scared woman at the door, her son, Jesse, and the other tribe members, how they would consternate before Mathias, the protector-in-chief. *He's an easy one to love,* thought Ray.

"Good afternoon," said Jerry, trying the friendly approach. Mathias stared and said nothing. "Glad we caught you here. We just came from Asa's…trying to place his last known location. Hopefully you can help us. We're coming up empty."

"Asa? What about him?"

"You live here alone?" Ray butted in to throw Mathias off for a moment. Jerry would be too straight to throw a curveball.

"Yes."

"Don't you have a big family? Eight siblings, something like that, and one of them, your brother, was killed?"

Mathias stared. Jerry stared. Ray had the floor.

"They live on the Cape," he said. "And my brother was shot in a robbery a long time ago. What's that got to do with anything? What are you here for?"

"You know what it's like to be mad, Mathias. Sounds like you were mad the town didn't give you the go ahead for the casino."

"Who is this guy?" Mathias shot a look at Jerry and pointed a trowel at Ray. "What the hell is this about?"

"Mathias, we want to talk to you about Asa. He's missing, and you were the last person we know to have seen him."

Mathias threw the trowel into the dirt. It stuck like a knife in tenderloin.

"I just had my building burn to the ground. I have a million in insurance claims up my ass. I've got a lot on my mind, Jerry, and this rent-a-cop bringing up my brother is bullshit."

Mathias turned to Ray, moved in close, eyes like ice picks nicking holes in his skull.

"You got a lot of nerve for a rent-a-cop."

Ray steadied his gaze, breathed out slow. His nose just about came up to Mathias's tan, vein-popped neck. It was a standoff—Big City Ray vs. Big Chief Mathias.

"You wanna see Asa, rent-a-cop? He's on the boat. Let's go."

———— ·•· ————

The three got into Mathias's truck and went to the harbor. Mathias had a thirty-five-foot Boston Whaler tied to the dock, rocking softly. A nice boat, too nice, for a humble chief of the people, for the people. Mathias took a key from his pocket.

"He's been in here for days. Showed up at my place high and hallucinating. Must be peyote spiked with something. He's totally off his nut. Cut off his own finger. Said it was infested with worms. He cut it off with one of my fishing knives and threw it in the water. I had to put him somewhere to keep him safe. What else could I do? I couldn't let him go and do more harm to himself."

"That's not your call to make," said Ray.

"And you are…?" shot back Mathias.

Ray didn't flinch. He was beyond flinching. Mathias had that cocksure attitude that let Ray slip into a cop bravado like a well-fitted dinner jacket.

"I could have you arrested on the spot for false imprisonment."

Mathias pushed a finger hard into Ray's chest. "You want to see him, rent-a-cop? I got other shit to do today."

Ray studied Mathias's face and channeled instinct, not logic. Ray felt the dead brother sob story wasn't tall enough to fill Mathias's enormous lifeforce with this much anger. The long braids, the dream-catcher abode, seemed like window dressing for a deep-rooted claim of sanctimonious privilege, to be Supreme Healer to his tribe for the never-forgiven evils: White Man's Genocide, the Church, Gifts of Small Pox. Ray wasn't buying it. He saw Mathias as a pissed off middle-aged guy who couldn't get what he wanted from life and took it out on everyone else.

Ray loathed Jerry in this moment too, for his silence.

Mathias boarded first, walked to the door of the hold, and put the key in the lock. A scuffing came from behind the door—clatter of stuff thrown around a room, then loud banging and screams.

"Open the door! Get me out. Get me out so I can kill you."

They heard Asa's fist hard and slow on the door, exhausted, desperate.

"Asa! I'm going to open the door. But the cops are here. They want to ask you some questions."

"Cops?" he said at last.

"They're investigating Nora's murder—the killing on Moshup's rock."

"No. I'm not talking to them." Asa's voice faded away from the door. "I'm not going. You brought them here. You'll lie and I say I did it. You'll tell them I'm crazy... I'm not going to prison. No."

Something solid hit the door inside. Mathias turned the key in the lock and pushed, but it didn't budge. He leaned in hard with his tremendous mass, shouldering the door open, finally bursting off a harpoon jammed up against it. Ray pushed into the small cabin behind Mathias just as a shot from a .22 caliber pistol cracked.

Asa's head hit the wall and made a wet, red trail down to where he stopped on the floor, his eyes dead and wide open. The pistol fell from his hand, the kind of pistol fishermen keep strapped to the wall for shooting tuna, sharks, and anything from the sea that wouldn't die nicely. Ray leaned over Mathias's shoulder and caught his first glimpse of Asa, splayed on the wall like a trophy fish.

CHAPTER 11
THE DRUGS

I T TOOK A WEEK FOR Busick to get around to sending the toxicology report for Nora to Jerry. When he got it, Ray saw him staring at the report like a kid about to fail a chemistry exam.

"You have some experience with this stuff, right? I need you to translate for me."

Ray scanned the multisyllabic names common enough in the dozens of overdose cases he'd worked until he came to "digitalis and glycosides." That didn't sound manmade. It sounded organic. And mescaline had been found in her as well—a hallucinogenic, hippy shit. It seemed Nora was a human pharmacy when she passed into the land of big sky.

"Well, Jer, our victim had a lot more than we suspected sloshing around in her veins. And what's surprising is this one I haven't heard of—digitalis purpurea."

They quickly searched Google and found it was the fancy way to say foxglove, a highly poisonous flower that could grow just about anywhere and looked good in a centerpiece. So how did Nora get it in her system? And what about the other narcotics?

Ray kept reading.

"It's unclear from this report what substance killed her. It's like someone was just throwing darts to see one hit bullseye."

"The only thing this does is reassure me we're not dealing with a professional."

"I'm going to agree with you. Whoever it is, or if it was Asa, they didn't know what they were doing. Still, the killer needed access to the narcotics. You can't grow those. And the mescaline, that's interesting. It's not going to kill you, just flip you out for a few hours. Wait, what did Mathias say on the boat? That he'd never seen anyone eat so much peyote before. What is that?"

Another quick search brought up a squat cactus full of mescaline, native to the Southwest US, that let you enter a personal fantasia. The Navajo called it peyote. That drug made sense—Ray could stretch to see Nora taking that. He pulled up the pictures from the morning they found Nora tied to the rock wearing the Native American clothes, the theater of it. Maybe it wasn't theater, and Nora was with others acting out a ceremony. That could account for the mescaline. And the other substances? Someone in the group shoots her full of narcotics and makes her eat deadly flowers? Or she eats the foxglove not knowing it's in something else, and then gets shot up?

Ray let out a grunt of frustration. "This report is getting us nowhere. We need to find out how all this garbage got in her system. We need to go back to her house and try to figure out what happened that night."

DEATH ON MOSHUP'S ROCK

"Should we tell Busick we're going back? What are we looking for?"

"You don't do peyote alone, Jer."

"You think Asa was at her house?"

"Asa is out of his mind high on peyote and who knows what else, cuts off his own finger, is an obvious danger to himself, is screaming to get off the boat. Then, as soon as we show up, he doesn't want to go…he would rather die than go to jail. That's a confession in my book. But of what, I don't know yet."

Ray was thinking out loud, winging it. The three motives for murder spun around his head like a roulette wheel—money, love, revenge—and one of them hit the right number.

"We overlooked something."

"What's that?" asked Jerry.

"A dumb kid is going to make a dumb mistake."

Jerry and Ray took a cruiser from Tisbury police station and headed up to Nora's place about an hour later. The windows down, both rode in silence. Ray glanced over at Jerry every few minutes, seeing his face twisting, mouthing a few words. Ray imagined Jerry turning over bizarre fantasies of Nora and Asa powwowing around Moshup's rock, high as kites, howling, chanting; something out of Dances with Wolves. He chuckled. Ray brought the toxicology report to read again, searching for a connection between the drugs. Foxglove, natural and could grow anywhere. Mescaline, from a very specific cactus in the Southwest. Narcotics, hard to get without a license. Two of the three won't necessarily kill you, and one would without the other two.

"You know, Jerry, one summer I came to a party out here, middle of nowhere, and this guy asks me if I want to smoke weed and I say, 'Yeah,' and then he asks me if I want to snort coke and I say, 'Yeah,' and then he asks me to get in the ocean naked and I say, 'Hell no.' I'm looking at this dude like, didn't you ever see *Jaws*? So he gets in the water and I'm staring at this bonfire and like a dozen drunk girls trying to pick one off when this big Samoan guy comes from behind the bonfire with a burning two-by-four in his hand, and I almost lost my shit. I thought this guy was going to murder someone."

Jerry pulled up to Nora's house, turning off the engine gently to not miss a word.

"So me being a dumbass, I go to tackle the guy, and he's a literal wall. I'm lying in the sand, flat on my back, with this huge guy looking down at me with a flaming two-by-four."

"Is there a connection? Was this guy someone we've questioned?" Jerry asked.

"Nah. It was just a crazy night." Ray laughed.

Nora's back door creaked open as it did before. This time Ray scanned the house, looking for something out of place, like the bedroom upstairs that was too neat, to indicate that someone else had possibly been there the day she died. Ray looked in the sink and there was a single knife, crusted with something like yellow cake. Ray took out his phone, snapped a pic, carefully lifted the knife with a gloved hand and dropped it into a plastic bag. On the counters were cans of dog food, really old bottles of vitamins, a jar of wheat germ, and a plate of corn bread—three big yellow squares. It was the only item on the counter not in a jar, can, or industrial packaging. Ray leaned over to sniff it. It smelled pretty good, like Anne could make. And it smelled recent. Maybe a few days. He snapped another pic, picked the plate up and slid the whole thing into a baggie.

"Jer, you ever go to any raging keggers around here?"

"I don't think so. But I like beer."

"I don't think our victim did either. Come check this out."

The center of the kitchen had a round wood table with four chairs, one tucked in and three pulled back. Anne's voice popped annoyingly into Ray's head, *"Who did she see up there in the woods?"*. Ray got down eye level to the table and looked across. Little yellow crumbs again. He got out a tweezer and picked up as many as he could see.

"I like beer too. We should go get banged up one night. Find a few honies. I can't believe forensics didn't get this, if they were ever here. I think our victim had a little party."

Ray snapped several pics of the table, chairs, counter, floors, door, sink, what was in the fridge and freezer. Then the two walked through the rest of the hobbit hole again, but nothing landed on their radar. Just for kicks, Ray looked under the bathroom sink again, thinking of how Anne would have snatched up Donna's engagement ring and palmed it.

Ray and Jerry walked around the house, looking for tire tracks, foot prints, some sign of who and how the visitors got there. Next to the house were two sets of bike treads, which could have made the party three for dinner.

Jerry leaned down next to Ray who was snapping a picture of the ground.

"Why would I ride a bike someplace, Jer?"

"It's good exercise?"

"My guess is you know you're going to be shitfaced in a few hours and don't want to risk getting pulled over."

"Too far to walk, I guess."

"Yup. And hitchhiking would place you near the scene."

"Any idea what kind of bikes?"

"Fat treads. I'm guessing all-terrain of some kind. Which means they might not have even come by a paved road. Damn it."

"We can put out a bulletin anyway just in case we have any eyewitnesses that saw two…people?…out riding that night."

"It's Asa, Jerry. Something tells me he was here. And who did Asa hang out with?"

"Mathias?"

"No, no. Buddies. Who would hang with the finger kid? Who do we know gets in trouble?"

"I'm guessing you know."

"The neighbor, Jesse."

"Did they use the bedroom…you know…and then make it neat?" Jerry could barely complete the sentence.

"Not a bad idea to pull the sheets for DNA. And we don't yet know how the McKenna ring got to the bathroom. Maybe our victim had more than one set of visitors."

"That ate corn bread?"

"Is the ring still in evidence?"

"Yeah, I filed the report and Busick said to hold the evidence because he was going to take care of it."

"He wants to keep the McKennas out of this. He wants to bury that. But we need to know how the ring got here. If Mrs. McKennna had it stolen then she would have reported it, which means she was probably wearing it here."

"I'm confused. Is the governor's wife our prime suspect? I thought it was Asa."

"It will be easy enough to trace Mrs. McKenna's movements. And maybe how she got here. If she came alone. The others are the mystery. The people who came on bikes."

"Who ate the corn bread, Ray?!"

"Hell if I know. My mom makes a great jalapeño corn bread. You need to try it."

Ray walked outside. It was a hot as hell night in July. The sweat was streaming down his back to the waistband of the blue cargo shorts he'd been wearing for weeks. Rent-a-cop. Summer hire. "Go back to the mainland" was all Ray felt from the moment he showed up. The chip on his shoulder was a canyon now. There wasn't another cop going to break this case, thought Ray, no way. Busick wasn't here, and he was dumb as boiled lobster anyway. The case was twisted in knots around Nora, and no one else was close to unraveling it.

"So, what's next?" Jerry asked.

"You're going to pull the sheets off the bed and bag them, seal the other evidence up and express them to the Boston lab. Look up corn bread recipes so we can compare them with what the lab sends back. Find out if Jesse or Asa rides a fat tire bike. Then call lazy ass Busick and

OK—

tell him we did his job. I'm off the clock as of ten minutes ago. I'm going to find a raging kegger."

Ray made his way back to town, hitchhiking, hoping to be picked up by a car of females in small shorts on their way to a beach party. Rather, a truck of refrigerated foods on its way to the Stop and Shop gave him a lift. It was going to be a long, dry summer.

Donna McKenna stared blankly into the bathroom mirror, tracing the lines on her face, padding the bags under her eyes with $120-per-ounce La Mer cream. Perfectly tanned, perfectly combed, perfectly dressed—she was going through the motions, doing what was expected of her. A daily cocktail of drugs—anti-anxiety, amphetamines, opioids—mechanized her muscles. Philip's soft touch had gotten her checked out of the hospital, but once back in Chilmark, he'd locked her away.

Donna became invisible, left out of gatherings and events, presented in press releases as absent due to a "delicate situation," which translated to a deep freeze. She rose each day, dressed impeccably, sat alone in the sunlit living room of stuffed fish and sailing trophies, and did nothing but listen to herself breathing.

Philip came into the bathroom. Her eyes watched him in the mirror. He had the hard set, cold look.

"I'm going to make a statement today about Henry and his ex-wife, the woman who was killed. There's new evidence he met with her. He's now a prime suspect."

"That's insane."

"Busick's been working this case. There's enough to hold Henry for questioning, which means he's off my staff."

"You bastard," she whispered. "You know he didn't do it."

"I want him away from you. I want this Indian business cleaned up."

"You're going to ruin him. His career is over if you let this happen."

"His career was over the moment you spread your legs, sweetheart. I knew the whole time. Your phony acts, the lies…you're like a pane of glass. I knew one of you would screw up eventually, I just had to wait."

Donna threw her makeup at the mirror and screamed. "You bastard. You don't love me, you never did!"

"You want to go to him now? He's done. I know you, you'll come crawling back when he can't find a job, when his contacts have dried up. You're weak, Donna, but you're not dumb."

"Get out! Get out!"

Red-faced, she slammed the door and slid to the floor. She sobbed into her hands, feeling the freshly applied face cream smear, little mascara droplets falling on her blouse. Life in Philip's cage was slowly starving her, fading her out until she was just a picture on his office desk, exactly as he wanted. She reached for the cabinet and opened the pill bottles. Shaking, she spilled them into the palm of her hand and ate them all before crawling into the tub.

"Please, dear God, someone help me," she whispered, and the World's #1 Trophy Wife closed her eyes, hopefully for the last time.

Rachel had her phone turned off. It was Sunday, she knew Dennis would be coming back tonight on the last boat, probably after driving for hours in traffic, and want to see her as soon as he arrived. Rachel also knew he had spent a long weekend with his wife, three kids, and in-laws, a situation that let her play the passive-aggressive vixen game. *To hell with that asshole*, she thought. *Let him come crawling on his knees, dripping with apologies. He'll have to beg to make it up to me. Then maybe I'll let him.*

Rachel's roommate looked out the window.

"He's here. Are you going to let him in?" she asked.

"Fuck no. Let him sit out there all night. Asshole."

Dennis beeped the horn, then again, and called to her through the moonroof.

"Can you just, please…" she asked.

"Oh my God, I'm not going down there."

The horn blared again. Dennis got out of the car, calling up to the window.

"Come on, baby, I drove four hours to see you."

Rachel came to the window and looked down to see Dennis in slender black shorts, a fitted gray T-shirt, a bottle of Veuve Clicquot and flowers, and his sexy-ass car gleaming in the streetlight. She gasped. A hot flash starting in her forehead traveled down her spine and back up again. She bit her lip and moaned, "Holy shit." Instantly, her body became a cat in heat. Any passive-aggressive strategy her brain concocted a few minutes ago to stab him in the heart just went out the window.

"Come on, baby. Let's go for a drive."

When she got down to the car, Dennis opened the door and she slid into the familiar seat. The dim lighting of the dash, the moonroof above. Dennis said nothing, kissing her softly again and again, drawing out her bitterness like the poison of a snake bite. She ran her long nails up the back of his neck and through his soft hair.

"I know where we can go," he grabbed her hand and put it on his thigh. She squeezed him hard and the car lurched into the street.

"Not your house. I don't want anything to do with that place."

"Sure, baby."

Rachel had rubbed most of the skin and hair off Dennis's thigh by the time he pulled into his office parking lot. Dennis kissed her hand and held it tightly as they went up the back steps, unlocked the office door and into a room. Rachel lay back on the exam table and the thin sheet of paper crinkled as he pulled down her shorts.

"You asshole," she whispered. And then laughed for the first time since he had left.

Donna was in the parking lot of Dennis's office. She had been for at least an hour, her engine running, staring into the nothingness. She watched Dennis and Rachel climb the stairs, the light coming through the window that was his exam room. She wished she was on that exam table in Dennis's office, sleeping forever under his care. Her body was pulsing with amphetamines and opiates, her heart giving off little explosions as the sweat poured from her hairline all over her clothes. Jaw clenched. Her chin dropped low on her chest and the world faded, then shot back with a bright clarity. She gripped the wheel to hold on to what reality was left as her mind slipped further behind those big sunglasses she wore even in the dark.

A figure approached. A knock on the car window.

"Mrs. McKenna. Are you okay?"

Donna was slumped on the steering wheel. The car engine was off.

Dennis tried the car door. Locked. He banged on the window. No response. Rachel watched from the top of the office stairs, watched him turn around with a look she had never seen before.

"Call 911, babe."

CHAPTER 12
THE WOODS

THE FIRST DAY OF AUGUST was a boiler, as if the sun had moved closer to the earth, and people actually got in the ocean to cool down. It was the kind of hot day that made you forget September was next, when cheap college labor left, summer rentals closed up, and guys working the to-go widow at Giordano's Pizzeria could lean on the counter and gab.

A week had passed since the fire. Andrew Cogswell, charged with arson, had been released from the county pen and sent home under house arrest to fish up a lawyer. The last pieces of the community center had been pulled to the ground by the fire department, and a few stray yards of DO NOT CROSS tape fluttered around. Mathias came by immediately after the fire to take pictures to send to the insurance company, to Amos "Little Drum" in Mashpee, to the Wampanoags who loved him, and the governor. Mathias squeezed the sympathetic organ to plan a rebuilding effort, enlisting supporters to post on social media and send ALL CAPS letters to town selectmen. Those who were overjoyed at the blazing, theatrical ending to a bad idea were equally annoying on their high horses, sneering into the editorial sections of the town papers. For a hot two weeks there was no more pressing topic on the minds of all islanders—whether and for what reason the Gay Head Community Center should be rebuilt. The vitriol raged on both sides and then, like a lunatic walking down the center of Main Street with a chainsaw that ran out of gas, it stopped. On the first day of August, islanders woke up to realize they had more pressing things to think about, such as squeezing every last dollar out of the season and hopefully breaking even.

The kitchen door was open when Ray walked up to the house on Juniper Lane. His mother jumped out of her seat.

"Finally. Come here. I have big news. Where've you been?"

"Working, Ma. There's this thing called texting. I know it's new to people of your generation."

"Listen. Guess who was brought to the hospital last night?"

"I have no idea."

"Come on, Ray. Use your brain. Why would someone call me and say, '*Guess who's in the hospital*'?"

"Because they're famous?"

"Now you're getting somewhere."

Anne loved these games, when she knew something that seemed so perfectly obvious to her and made the rest of the world out as plain stupid.

"A celebrity visiting the island?"

"The governor's wife," said Anne as she slapped the table. "I knew there was something wrong with that woman. She's trapped with that damn big-shot husband, probably tried to overdose to take out her last revenge on him. She wants his career to go down in flames. What did I tell you? I know a rotten marriage when I see it."

"Wait, wait. How do you know it's her and how do you know it's a drug overdose?"

"Susan called me. Her son is an EMT, and he drove her to the hospital, *alone*."

The red flare of Donna McKenna shot into the dark sky of Ray's mind again, and this cry for help, if it was an overdose, was much more over-the-top than the fainting episode at the golf club.

"Susan also told me her son picked her up once before, at the Harbor View, because she collapsed or something. I'm telling you, that woman is not long for this earth."

Anne pulled up her knee and put her hand on her kerchief, rocking back in her chair, sucking on her teeth. "Yup, she's saying, 'To hell with you people, I want out.'"

"Well, I've got bigger news than that. Henry Ammons is now the prime suspect for Nora's murder. Busick dropped the bomb with Jerry, and the Tisbury Police and Boston PD are coming to get him. They want to take Henry back to Boston for questioning. Apparently Henry was the last person to see Nora alive. At least the last person they know about."

"Well, that's convenient. Get rid of the lover, put the wife in her place. Now *that* makes sense." Anne beamed.

"There's got to be more to it, Ma."

"Don't overthink it, Ray. People are not that smart. Especially politicians."

Ray's phone buzzed. It was Jerry.

"You'll never guess who asked for you, Ray. Henry Ammons. Can you come to the station?"

———— •••• ————

Ray had met Henry only once, when they shook hands at Nora's funeral. In his sharp black suit, carrying a bouquet, he was a dapper, well-cut guy.

That was last month. Ray met an older Henry at the station—dark circles under his eyes, breath of Listerine and whiskey. He was sweaty and flushed, like a man who'd been out running and drinking, and then just drinking.

"Thanks for meeting, Ray. We met before, if you remember."

Jerry tried to play a strong hand and jumped in before Ray could respond. "Tell us why you're here."

"I'm here because I'm innocent. I know that's what you expect me to say, but it's true. I want to help clear up my ex-wife's murder. I was suspended from my job, which means I'm basically done, finished. You don't survive this in my business. I was supposed to go to Boston today for questioning and then…then Mrs. McKenna…" Henry's voice stopped, he wiped his hands with his face, breathing out hard. "She died in the hospital last night from a drug overdose."

Ray bit his lip to keep from talking. *Let Henry keep going*, he said to himself. *Let the picture paint itself.* But Jerry didn't have that coloring book.

"Okay, that's a shock," said the officer, "but what does that have to do with you and Nora's murder?"

Ray jumped in. "Oh man, I'm so sorry. You two were…close."

Henry crumbled into his hands. He had watched the woman he loved fall apart in front of him and wasn't able to do a thing about it. Ray put a hand on his shoulder and let the guy sob it out for a minute. And in that minute, Ray gleaned what he could from millions of years of mankind loving and hating and breeding and killing. *Don't overthink it, Ray,* he told himself. *Don't overthink why Henry is here.*

"I was supposed to go to Boston but now I'm going to be questioned here. The governor is flying her home. He said to keep my distance. Out of respect, he says. I didn't kill Nora. I had no reason to. Donna and I used her house when it was empty. That's all. Now Donna's gone, my career is done. I need a way out of this. I need to prove I'm not a killer."

"I get it, man. What can you tell us about your ex-wife that we don't know?"

Henry paused. His eyes went dead, fixed on some vision, maybe of Donna, maybe of Nora, maybe of max-security hell. He had stopped breathing, and then came back with a snap.

"She told me to stop the casino. To tell the governor to quash the whole thing. She knew that Donna and I were having an affair. To her, that was leverage."

"Did anyone else know this?"

"Donna knew it. She was there when Nora made the threat."

"That gives you motive, Henry. Nora knew about you and Donna."

"I didn't kill her, damn it."

"Did you tell the governor about Nora's threat?"

"No. I knew the whole casino thing was a shell game. It was a cheap PR move to appease some big donors and distract people from the real money maker, a megacasino called Two Feathers being built on the Cape. So I kept my mouth shut and hoped it would blow over with her, with Nora. She can run hot and cold. One day she's sweet and the next day she wants to burn the place down."

"Do you know who wanted to kill Nora? Did she have any enemies?"

"She could get really committed to ideals and not hold back. We marched once for PETA and threw bricks at a fur store window. That was as close as I ever came to being arrested, before this."

"Can you think of anyone specific? Do you know why she would be dressed in Indian clothes and tied to a rock that said 'Moshup'?"

"Nora was a very serious person. She wouldn't have dressed that way as a joke. I've racked my brain about this. She would only put that on if she was with other serious people."

"Other Wampanoags?"

"Probably."

Ray leaned back in his chair and chewed his lip.

Jerry the Spectator was finishing a bag of Cape Cod potato chips he found in a drawer five minutes ago.

"If she was that against the casino, could she have made herself the enemy of those who wanted it?"

"Absolutely."

Ray looked over at Jerry, mid chip. "This sounds like bad blood. A Podunk bingo joint isn't worth it unless it's personal. I think we know where to start, Jer. With our old pal Mathias."

"Oh yeah, and that reminds me, the bikes!" Jerry exclaimed. "Both Asa and Jesse have bikes with tire treads that are a match to the ones by Nora's house."

"So you have other suspects?" Henry asked eagerly.

"We think two others came on bikes, who live up near there. They came by but we don't know why. One guy is dead. The other is bad news."

"Nora had a soft spot for troubled youth. Maybe she was trying to help them. We never had any kids. She had issues with her parents that made her, well, hate them, and she felt guilty and got involved with youth programs or something. This is going back more than ten years."

"Oh yeah, and that also reminds me, Henry," Jerry said, "you need to give your DNA. And do you eat corn bread?"

"Corn bread? Sure."

"Spicy corn bread?" Jerry leaned in with bulging eyes.

Ray interrupted. "Nora had it in her stomach. It was the last thing she ate before she died that morning, along with a cocktail of toxins."

"I think you've got some leads." Henry turned to Ray. "And I want to help you however I can."

Ray paced around the small office. Something itched his brain.

"You said the Gay Head casino was a cheap PR move. That there's a bigger project on the Cape that's the real deal. Why does the governor care?"

"Because he's the bank roll for Two Feathers. I thought you guys knew that."

CHAPTER 13
THE TRIANGLE

ASA'S BLOOD HAD BEEN CLEANED off the Boston Whaler, his body bagged, sent to the morgue. An open-and-shut suicide case. Three witnesses. There was no reason Mathias couldn't get back to his boat and to fishing, now that he had nothing to do but wait. He had assurances, promises from the governor, from Mashpee, that the Phoenix of Gaming would rise and the casino would happen, just delayed for one more summer.

Mathias pulled up to Jesse's house, a bright, cheerful little thing surrounded by flowers and vegetables, kept by the tiny June Vanderhoop. A slight woman, she reached her son's shoulder and just about Mathias's chest plate, but she had ferocious blue eyes, not the expected soft brown to match her long hair and dark complexion. Mathias watched her turn slowly from her gardening and stare blankly at him. He never liked her.

Jesse was flinging fishing poles around in a shed, yelling something about his mother throwing stuff away and why was this place such a disorganized dump, he couldn't find anything. Mathias descended from his truck to load the fishing gear thrown on the ground onto the flatbed.

June's cold blue eyes watched him, her face slack without emotion, like an Indian doll sold to tourists. Finally she spoke. "I know you want to take my son fishing. He told me this morning, and I made a special basket of food to take."

"Don't eat anything she makes. Her food is gross," Jesse yelled from the shed, now pulling tackle boxes off the shelves, one spilling onto the shed floor. He left it there.

"I made it for you, Mathias. My son only eats potato chips." She tried a smile.

"We are going out to Cuttyhunk and spend the day. I think Asa shooting himself is a lot for Jesse to take in. It is for all of us."

June took a step toward Mathis and lowered her voice. "You have taken my son under your wing like a father. Jesse never had a father. He left us when my son was a baby. You knew that when we came to this reservation. My son will do anything for you."

Mathias looked down at the tiny woman, hearing her thin-veiled insinuations. Yes, he had taken in Jesse, given him odd jobs, kept him out of jail, given him money when he needed it, filled his head with ambitions. Mathias became the everything Jesse never had, and it drove a blunt wedge between mother and son. Jesse would do anything for Mathias and Mathias knew it, wanted it, needed it.

June handed Mathias the basket of foods she made with herbs from her garden—a garden of traditional Wampanoag plants used for healing the mind, the body, the spirit. Mathias tossed it on the back seat and started the truck. Jesse sucked on his vape and cranked up Bob Seger on the radio singing about some old time rock and roll.

Seven and Seven out of Oak Bluffs was rounding the tip of Gay Head beach. Captain Rodney, shirtless in a white jacket and matching short shorts straight out of 80's *Love Boat,* chewed an unlit stogie, soft and salty as a pretzel. In what's called a poor life choice, he invited too many raucous forty-somethings on his Sea Ray Sundancer to cruise to Cuttyhunk, an even smaller island than Martha's Vineyard, to see the world's smallest post office. In his jaunty captain's hat, Rodney gunned the outboards, and the boat, well over its weight limit, lifted heavily out of the water, crashing hard into the waves. The women screamed, their hair flying all over their heads. The guys pumped their fists into the air. Everyone was three sheets to the wind as the sound system blasted Metallica. It was noon.

As the boat topped the curve of Gay Head, some of the guys shouted to come in close to the naked beach under the cliffs. The women rolled their eyes. Captain Rodney slowed down and handed one of the guys binoculars.

"Here. Christ. It's all old tits."

And then another thing caught Rodney's attention, a Boston Whaler akilter, grazing against a line of rocks called Devil's Bridge, which even intoxicated Rodney knew enough to avoid. There was no one onboard that he could see, and the bow bobbing against the rocks must have been creating a huge gash. He idled the engine, snatched the binoculars back, and took a look. In the Whaler, across the bench seat a man was slumped, passed out. There didn't seem to be anyone else on board.

"What's up, oh, Captain, my Captain?" asked a passenger.

"I think I gotta make a call. Shit, I'm overlimit. Let's hope the Coast Guard doesn't care, or some of you idiots are swimming."

"Not in this Jaws-infested water."

"Just shut up and sit tight. I'll be back in a minute."

Rodney went below and picked up the radio to call the CG. It was not a call he wanted to make, but if he didn't and his boat was later identified as in the area, he could be in for a lot of extra questions and a few thousand in fines.

"This is *Seven and Seven*, reporting a vessel in distress. Medical assistance might be needed too. Looks like a guy is passed out on board."

After a few minutes, Rodney came back.

"All right, party people, we gotta hang here for a minute."

"What's the deal?"

The other guy took up the binoculars again and stared at the boat. They had drifted even closer, and it was now clear that the person on the Boston Whaler was not moving.

"That's a big guy. That doesn't look good. Why do we have to hang around?"

"Just sit and have a drink. There goes my fucking day," sighed Rodney.

"Can I see?" one of the women asked. "I'm a nurse, so maybe…"

She looked over for a long minute. The whole boat was silent, rocking heavily in the waves. Then she put the binoculars down.

"That man is dead. I can see his face is blue and there is vomit all over the seat and the floor. And I think I know who it is. It's the Indian guy that wants to build the casino place."

The news of Mathias's vomitous death at sea spread fast. The nurse texted her friend, who texted six others, who posted something on social media, and before the CG could get the boat towed back to harbor, every device on the island buzzed eighteen times with the same picture of the boat plus the cruel, indelicate, comedic commentary that only comes with anonymity. Via six degrees of separation, it finally reached Ray, who was going through his mother's mail.

"Holy crap."

"What?" Anne sat up, fanning herself with a flyer for Cronig's market. Half off chicken.

"Mathias might be dead."

"You're kidding! How do you know?"

"Someone texted me, and it's on Instagram."

"What's that?"

"It's illegal is what it is, and shocking. Mathias. Wow. He was our prime suspect."

"Well, now you got problems."

Ray shook his head at Anne's obvious and insulting comment. Back to Ammons as their lead? Ray's phone rang, it was Jerry.

"Ray, you're not going to believe it."

"Mathias is dead. Yeah, it's blowing up social media."

"How did you…? Never mind. I don't do that stuff. The Coast Guard recovered his boat, and he was dead for a few hours, it seemed."

"No one else aboard when it happened?"

"Nope. But it's also not really their job to look. I think you—uh, we need to go see the boat."

"Already on my way."

Jerry and Ray arrived separately, walked to the harbor where the Whaler was being lifted to dry dock. With a five-foot gash in the hull, she wouldn't have lasted long. Jerry went to talk to the CG captain while Ray snapped a few pics.

"Well, lookie lookie," Ray said to himself.

Leaning on a wall, watching with no particular interest, was Andrew Cogswell, sucking on a long-neck beer. So much for house arrest. The man was a local hero.

Ray stared at him for a while. Drew didn't look nervous or bothered or particularly anything. Just a guy with all the time in the world for watching whatever there was to watch going on on his island.

Jerry trotted back, saw Ray staring at Drew.

"Well, whaddayaknow?"

"Yeah, and he doesn't look terribly shaken," said Ray. "But we should go talk to him."

"The CG wants to know if we want to go through what's on the boat, including some food. There's corn bread on board. Do you believe it?"

"Is that a joke, Jer? 'Cause it's good."

"Mathias is being kept at MV Hospital but not for much longer. The medic says it looks like poisoning."

Ray hadn't taken his eyes off Drew, who recognized Jerry and was now staring back. Ray's brain itched again.

"Jer, with Mathias dead, who wins? The casino was a ruse, the town dodges the bullet, the tribe gets Two Feathers, and the governor we assume gets the win. It's all tied up so nice. So who still wants Mathias dead? How is this connected to Nora's murder? And what about the John Doe on the slab in the basement? Are we sure there was no one else on board?"

Jerry looked around, then held a finger to his lips and made a shushing sound. He pointed to the boat with a big thumb and nodded. Ray chuckled at how much he loved this man.

The Whaler was in dry dock—the CG had their once-over, stuck police tape on it, and moved on. Jerry and Ray snapped on some rubber gloves and climbed up the stern ladder. The deck smelled of bile and fish bait. Ray looked at the table where Mathias croaked it and noticed red smudges.

Next, he opened the door to the hold that Asa had been trapped in for days and went down to the small galley and berth. The fishing gear and harpoon were still there. The long red streak from Asa's gunshot had been cleaned off a while ago, when the boat was released back to Mathias. Open-and-shut suicide. Nothing fancy. Now there was new blood, fresh as wet paint. It smeared the wall in a palm print.

"Looks like interested party number two was here. So where are they now? Overboard?"

"This isn't Mathias's blood?"

"No, he bit it up on the deck. And from poison. Either Mathias was shaving in the chop or putting the chop to someone else."

The floor was a mess of plastic plates, cups, plastic wrap, and incredibly, yellow crumbs. Ray picked up a few and dropped them in a baggie. Then he snapped some pics of the blood-smeared wall, the floors, the deck, the seat.

"Itty bitty crumbs, Jer. Hansel and Gretel were here."

"Ray, we need Dukes County, or your Boston department. We need that forensics team to figure out what happened here. I don't have the stomach for this anymore."

"Yeah, they'll be camping here soon, and Busick will be all over it. But it won't do any good. The person we're looking for isn't in the directory. I told you, dumb kids will do dumb stuff."

"What kid?"

"Jesse."

Jerry leaned against the wall, and sighed. Ray patted him on the arm and climbed down the stern ladder. Drew was gone, the harbor was dark.

"We've got more work to do tonight, Jer," he said as he got into his mom's white Volvo, making sure not to get blood on her seats.

———————————————

The reservation streets had no lights, only dim slices of light coming from under window shades. They drove past the scorched black spot that was the rubble of the community center to the cluster of houses.

Asa's house was still dark. Jesse's house next door looked alive, maybe. Jerry and Ray climbed out of their cars, Jerry with no idea of the game plan, Ray improvising. They knocked.

The same blank face with blue eyes answered the door as before, unmoved. Ray leaned on the door a bit and saw a simple house with the tv on too loud.

"Good evening. Remember us? Tisbury Police. Is Jesse here?"

The blank face shook no, an unexpectedly calm shake for two official-looking guys on the doorstep at night.

"We came to see if he's all right. We think he might be hurt."

The blank face might have twitched, but it was dark. Ray leaned on the door. He could see a dimly lit room but no other occupants.

"Mind if we come in? We have just a few questions."

Jesse's mom stepped backward, hand still on the knob, and finally spoke.

"He's not here."

"You're his mother, correct?"

Silence.

"June Vanderhoop, correct?"

"He's not here."

"Are you sure? When did you see him last?"

Ray, carried by the scent of something cooking, looked over her shoulder into the kitchen. On the counter he could see various pans stacked.

"Mind if we take a look around anyway?" Ray overpowered her, gently, and walked into the house.

June ran into the kitchen and stood in front of them. "I told you he's not here."

Ray noticed the pans were recently used and crusted with yellow. "What did you make in the pan?"

"Nothing. My grandmother's recipe."

"We need this for evidence." Ray reached for the pan.

June twisted quickly and slid a knife from the wood-block. She lifted her hand high above her shoulder and with a thrust down stabbed Ray deep in the hand. He howled, blood splattering up into his face on the counter and floor as he pulled away. She swung high at him again and he grabbed her wrist with his good hand and pulled her to the floor. She screamed and kicked like a wild horse, slamming her heel into Ray's knees and shin. She wrapped her legs around Ray and pulled him down with surprising force, twisting her body like a corkscrew. Jerry went down to restrain her and all three were on the floor now, Ray's hand gushing making the floor slippery with his blood as he reached for the knife a few inches away. June fought for it too, but Jerry had the longer reach and flicked it away from her across the linoleum floor, streaking red. It hit a shoe and stopped.

Jesse was silently watching the three of them, a bandaged arm at his side, his face expressionless. He made no move to disentangle his mother or pick up the knife.

"Run!" June screamed, and then something else that neither Ray nor Jerry understood. She screamed it again, and Jesse bolted from the house. Jerry and Ray scrambled after him, but June reached for their legs and pulled them hard to the floor again. She slammed her fist on top of Ray's bloody hand, and he screamed in pain. Jerry, finally up, yanked June's hands behind her back, grabbed the handcuffs off his belt and left her face down on the dirty floor. Ray ran out the door but didn't see a thing. It was pitch black, no streetlights, no moon. He walked back into the kitchen and wrapped his hand in a dishtowel.

"Grab those pans and bag them, Jer. Get her in your cruiser. Fuck, my hand hurts."

CHAPTER 14
EVERYTHING PERFECT IS FULL OF FLAWS

J ESSE'S PHONE WAS RUNNING LOW, but he opened it anyway to see the pictures on social media of Mathias dead on the boat. He had managed to swim to shore, slip back into his house unnoticed, and wrap his hand before the cops came. Now his hand was throbbing, bleeding through the bandage and he hugged it close to his chest as he walked. He'd walked for miles it seemed, guided through the darkness by dull memories, to get to the name his mother had screamed. It annoyed Jesse that he was going there. It was a retreat further into the world he didn't want to be a part of, that he never understood since he could remember. But his hand pulsed with pain, he was tired, and the only two people he had ever trusted were dead.

It was an old house, set deep in the woods without a road. It had a horror-movie abandoned look to it, as if it had been dropped from a dark sky and forgotten. An odor of damp and rot hung in the air, making it feel cold. Two windows and a small wooden door. Jesse raised his good hand and knocked. There was a shuffle and after a minute the stuck door slid open a few inches, stopped, and, with a lot of effort from the person inside, slid a few more. Jesse looked into the face and the face looked back, a good head shorter, shriveled and small. The head nodded, barely, and let Jesse come inside.

"Let me see your hand," she asked.

"Don't touch me."

"I've been waiting for you to come, waiting for a long time. June wants you to stay here. We will figure out what to do."

"What if I don't. You going to put a spell on me, you witch?"

She sighed and, leaning on a cane, shuffled to an old chair, fell heavily into the cushion, and stared forward at nothing.

"She tried so hard for you. She has a good soul but you are too much. She knows she lost you a long time ago."

Jesse stood near the door, wanting to leave but not moving, paralyzed by the nothingness of dark woods at his back and his disgust for the world he was in.

"She's just as stupid as you. Mathias was the only one who ever wanted to…to do anything. I've been stuck in this place forever watching the freak show festivals of yours that never made a difference and made us look like dancing idiots."

The voice went on softly without listening. "She sacrificed everything to protect you…from yourself, from him. Now she will be gone. And Mathias, your false leader, is also gone. You are alone."

"So why am I here, huh? Why did she tell me to come here, you goddamn witch?"

"You will be safe here. We will take care of you. And we will destroy this together."

A drawer opened. Jesse recognized the syringe and vial he used on Nora. The drugs to keep her quiet, to keep her in line. His eyes locked on it.

"June took this from your room and gave it to me. She knew what Mathias asked you to do. She was desperate to stop you from throwing your life away. Don't you understand…? You killed Nora, yes, but your mother… she tried to kill Nora first. With foxglove. She knew you wouldn't eat anything she made. Nora would. She might eat enough to die before you could do what Mathias wanted. Then she poisoned your precious Mathias to make sure he would never tell."

Jesse snatched the vial with his good hand. His other hand throbbed inside the bandage, now black with congealed blood. Throbbing. Throbbing. Time slowed. He stood over her and looked down, feeling a hot swell of anger take over his body.

"No," he whispered. "You're just a fucking witch."

He hit her to the floor and walked out into the nothingness.

———

The darkness, the woods, went on and on, unending. Jesse wandered through the thick underbrush below and the pine trees above that kept out the stars. He wandered, a hungry and beaten animal without a home or a destination. His arm was numb and he hugged it to his chest, clenching the vial in his good hand. He remembered what Mathias had said, the lie that the drug was a psychedelic to scare her, or silence her, or tranquilize her. Jesse had been played, played like a calf-skin drum, for the pleasure of another.

In the distance, he heard mechanical whirring and walked toward the sound. After a few minutes, he discovered he was in a cow pasture, the sound was the milking machines pulsing away. The faint orange of dawn was just breaking over the tops of the trees, and he could see the farmhands working. Trucks and tractors were starting up, heading toward a road on the other end of the pasture. Jesse slipped behind a barn and waited for his opportunity.

A milk truck slowly bounced down the dirt road, and Jesse used all the strength in his one good arm to grab the tailgate and climb in. He lay flat and breathless, waiting for the driver to notice, but the truck went on, hit the main road, and turned.

Feeling emboldened by his stunt, Jesse's adrenaline kicked in and he got an idea. Mathias never told him or Amos where he got the drug, but Jesse had gone to court often enough to know the local suppliers. He looked closely at the small vial, with no markings or label except "MV Hospital use" printed across the glass.

Rachel was stretching across Dennis's desk like a cat napping in the sun, lazily raising her green eyes to him. His hands gripped her thighs and pulled her in closer, sliding all the papers off the desk to the floor. Rachel had come in with a stack of scripts for him to sign, dropped her chin and her voice to a sultry register, and stretched over the desk. He'd taken her up on her offer and pushed his next appointment out a few more minutes. The stack of scripts fluttered to the floor, and Rachel bent suggestively to pick them up, then stacked them like a deck of cards back on the desk. She blew him a kiss and closed the door.

Back at her desk computer, she reviewed her shopping cart items: a white bikini, straw bag and matching shoes, a necklace of huge saltwater pearls. After August wrapped and the season was over, she was sure Dennis would take them to Bermuda, just as they had talked about. He couldn't go any sooner as his calendar was full, and a full calendar meant his practice, and her life, was flush.

The back door opened and shut, but she didn't bother to turn around. She was reconsidering if the white bikini was as exciting as a black one. It was probably a delivery, or Dennis going to his car. Then she heard footsteps to Dennis's office, and the door open and close. Rachel was now curious as to who would just walk in without an appointment or through the lobby.

She put her ear to Dennis's office door.

"I want ten thousand dollars. I know this is from you," said a strange voice.

Then Dennis's response, "What makes you think I'd give you ten thousand, for that?"

"Ten is not a lot to stay silent."

"Silent for what?"

"This came from you. It says hospital use. You get your drugs there. You sold it to Mathias. Or your assistant did. I know she works there."

A pause.

"I don't keep money in the office."

"Then pills. Oxy." The voice got louder, more desperate.

Rachel was frozen outside the door. She had no idea what the stranger was talking about and why it would be worth so much to keep silent.

She knocked cautiously. "Everything okay in there?"

"Yes, Rachel, we're fine. Can you find me the keys to the Rx cabinet, please?"

Rachel went back to her desk to get the keys when a familiar face walked into the lobby.

"I like you better in your hospital coat. Is the doctor in?" Ray winked.

"Uh," she whipped her head around to look back at the doctor's office door, then at Ray, and now another police officer who entered the lobby. Her heart sank into her stomach.

Down the hall, the sound of grunting and struggling, and then the doctor's office door burst open. Jesse sprinted down the hall and out the back, down the steps to the parking lot. Ray immediately recognized him, flew down the hall, and chased after him but got his shirt caught on the long door handle, pulling Ray in a twist, giving Jesse just enough headway to run like a rabbit across the parking lot into dense trees.

"Damn it. Sawyer! Call for backup. That's our guy," Ray shouted back down the hall.

Sawyer was busy in Dennis's office, putting his hands in cuffs, reading him his rights.

"This is the guy we came here to get. The kid can wait. And I'm going to need to talk to you too, miss."

Rachel, shocked, breathless against the wall, watched a stoic Dennis get cuffed. He completely ignored her as he brushed past and Sawyer lead him out of his office.

"I can't...I can't believe you did this to me. I can't believe I was so stupid," she whispered to herself, collapsing into tears on his desk, the pile of scripts fluttering to the floor.

And the silent doctor walked out into the nothingness.

The governor's orders, relayed through Busick to Tisbury Police, were to arrest Dennis the pill pusher who'd flushed little Donna McKenna like a goldfish down the toilet. Ray seeing Jesse there was a bonus since they had lost all trace of him since the night before.

Ray called Jerry at the station, eager for the chase to go on, to arrest his suspect, to hopefully get his Boston PD job back before the fall.

"Jerry, he was here, I chased him. Jesse was here at the doc's. We need some backup—he's on foot, so we can probably catch him."

"That's good to know, Ray. We have backup to spare. Your old boss, Busick, is here. With your mother."

"What?"

"I think he wants to talk to..."

Busick ripped the phone away from Jerry and spit his Boston brogue. "I heard you missed me, so I came back."

"Yeah, I missed you so much I did your job for you. When are you gonna get some people down here? He's our prime suspect and he can't be that far."

"Stop playing cop, Ray. It's Ammons we're looking at."

"That's not gonna hold up and you know it. Ammons pissed off your boss and sent you to make his life miserable. Ammons didn't kill Nora. He didn't kill anyone. And no one gave a damn about the two-bit casino. But you knew that."

"Look, we've got our suspect and you're off the job. You never should have been on it."

"Ray! Just do what he says to get your job back," his mother's voice sailed in the background.

"What is she doing there?" Ray asked himself out loud.

"Your mother came down here looking for you. She's a real ball of fire." Busick snorted.

"Ray, get over here and tell these people what you know. You straighten this out," Anne shouted.

"Ma'am, can you please not yell while I'm on the phone?" Busick had all the restraint of a leashed attack dog.

"Don't you tell me what to do! I'm a widow! My son is a police officer on disability!"

A thought itched Ray's brain. "Do you still have the McKenna ring? Let her look at it. Guaranteed it will shut her up."

Busick snapped his fingers. "Jerry, get the McKenna bag. Give it to her."

Some shuffling noise, then silence. Ray smiled to himself.

"All right, what's your bright idea about this other guy? Make it quick."

"Come down here to the Spahr office and help me find Jesse. He and Asa murdered Nora. And get some people to arrest June Vanderhoop for the murder of Mathias."

"That's a load of crap."

"And our John Doe is just a casualty of the sea."

Busick's bull-headed breath fuzzed into Ray's ear. "You got some 'splaining to do."

Ray walked around the parking lot, waiting on Busick and Jerry. June's knife did a job on his hand, and he took two painkillers from his pocket. He held them in his palm for a minute, then threw them on the ground and crushed them with his heel. *Suck it up and deal with it*, he told himself.

The black Escalade pulled into the parking lot. Busick slid out and slammed the door. His red face glistened with sweat. He was pissed. He came back to the island from Boston to pick up Ammons and shut the book on "My Very Vineyard Summer" and found Ray Cillo chaffing at him like sand in a bathing suit. Busick snapped off his Oakleys and looked like a rabid raccoon.

"Well?"

"Your doc's in the cruiser over there, but he's not talking. Making deals on the governor's behalf is your specialty, so maybe you can get something out of him."

"Watch yourself, cowboy." Busick went over to the cruiser and tapped on the window. The doc didn't move and only said he wanted his lawyer.

The tinted back window of the Escalade dropped, and Anne stuck half her body out, arms waving.

"Ray! Come see this!!"

Ray froze, eyes wide. His mother was the one person who he didn't anticipate, couldn't control, and couldn't get rid of. She was shaking a plastic bag in her hand.

"Oh my God, she brought it," Ray muttered.

Ray walked to the Escalade, watched his mother dig a jeweler's loop from her enormous purse and shove it at Ray's face.

"Here, look. Even through the plastic I can see it's full of flaws. Just like I told you. No stone that big is perfect."

"That's great, Ma. I'm so glad you got to see it up close. Now please put that evidence bag someplace safe."

"Just like their picture. So perfect, and underneath, full of flaws. She's dead. Her husband got rid of her and her boyfriend just like I said would happen. And now your old boss wants to bring in the boyfriend for killing his ex-wife? Let me tell you, after that many years, you've moved on."

"I agree with you. I know it's within the tribe."

"You mean Indians killing Indians?"

"Yeah, Mathias had it in for anyone who would oppose him. Nora had a history as an organizer, and he sent the two to persuade her and, if that didn't work, scare her. Maybe he told them what the stuff would do, maybe he didn't and they got overzealous. Asa lost it after he found out Nora was dead and ate so much peyote he went out of his mind and then shot himself. Jesse was also scared, probably went back to Mathias to get protection, and that backfired too. Mathias took him out on the boat, probably tried to wound him and throw him overboard to drown but two things went wrong. Jesse is a great swimmer and

Mathias ate too much of a spicy corn bread dish that's popular right now."

Busick was standing behind Ray, listening intently, trying not to look like he was listening intently. Jerry was next to Busick, mouth agape.

"June Vanderhoop's special recipe goes heavy on the digitalis purpurea, also known as foxglove. It grows all over the island. In large quantities it can make you extremely sick, even kill you, which is what June Vanderhoop hoped to do to Nora, and then Mathias."

Busick leaned into Ray. "Why don't you 'splain that a bit more for Jerry, who's too tardy to see the whole picture."

"June Vanderhoop had a strong feeling her son, her out-of-control son, was doing Mathias's bidding to shut up Nora. June got in front of it as best she could to knock off Nora before Asa and Jesse got stupid, but it wasn't enough. Nora ate the poison but the drugs did the job. Then she made another batch to kill off Mathias before Mathias could kill off Jesse. That time she put in enough foxglove to do the job."

"Who's this?" Anne asked.

"June Vanderhoop," the three men, in unison.

"Don't yell. Of course she did. Any mother would do that for her child. Imagine how guilty she felt for failing her son. What are you living for if you can't stop your child from self-destruction? Did you figure all that out yourself, Ray? That's good."

"Jesse going to the doc's office also means he knew, or took a risky bet, the drugs came from Spahr. I doubt Spahr knew what the drug was for when he sold it. Either way, he didn't want our stumpy to ruin a good pill-pushing racket."

"Now I gotta find me a new doctor. Too bad. Good-looking guy."

Busick pinched his lips and then moved them slowly. "What about the bingo hall? Cogswell burning that to the ground is not connected to the murder?"

"Drew Cogswell is a lifelong islander who sees himself as a vigilante of justice. He'll probably get time but I guarantee he'll be elevated to epic status as a martyr. What you don't get, Busick, with your off-island boat drink jokes, is this place…it's a tug of war between people who hate the outside world and people who keep pulling it in closer."

"That's right." Anne leaned in. "They built this huge roundabout so they wouldn't have to have a stop light. So a few people crash their cars. Who cares."

"It's a love-hate world on this island," Ray continued. "People like Cogswell, Nora, everyone who hates the idea of a casino, they think they're the protectors."

Busick frowned, shrugged his shoulders. "Get the Vanderhoops if you want. I get Ammons in my personal fishbowl."

"Jerry, let's go on down to Mathias's place on Moshup's Trail. Huh. Coincidence?"

"What?"

"Moshup. That's what was on the rock. Could have come to mind because that's where Mathias lived. Subconsciously we do things and leave a trail without knowing. Should have seen that."

"Now you're using your brain," Anne beamed. "Christ, it's hot. How long you gonna stand out there?"

And she rolled up the window. Jerry, Busick, and Ray watched their reflection come up slowly in the black tint.

"Your mom is the most interesting person I've ever met," said Jerry with an honest face.

Ray smirked. "Come on, Jer, we have to get moving before it's dark and we lose him a second time. Ten bucks says he's going to Mathias's to see what he can scrounge."

"Get me some rub-offs on the way," Anne shouted through the glass.

———•••———

The Ford F-150 was missing from Mathias's house. That was the first thing Ray noticed as he walked up in silence with Jerry. They'd left the cruiser back on the main road.

The door was open, the house quiet. Not much in it. On a wall, a shotgun mount was empty.

"If this kid would stop doing stupid stuff for five minutes, we might be able to help him," muttered Ray.

Jerry's phone buzzed. The harbormaster of Menemsha sent a pic and description of a guy fitting Jesse's description walking on and off boats. Looking for someone, maybe.

Jerry called him back and put the phone on speaker.

"Can you describe him?"

"Oh, midtwenties, maybe. One hand is in a bandage. He's got a rifle."

"Please keep away from him."

"He's boarding another boat. Hey!" The call cut off.

———•••———

It was an eight-minute drive from Moshup's Trail to Menemsha Harbor—if you obeyed the speed limit. Ray pushed the cruiser around corners and made it in four. Jerry gripped the door handle in silence.

The harbor looked still, just a few docked fishing boats, a few pleasure cruisers. Ray sprang from the car and into the harbormaster's office.

"Is he still here?"

A bony finger that smelled of fish bait pointed to the end of the dock. There was Jesse, shotgun tucked under his arm, skulking between boats, looking in windows and on the decks. Ray walked slowly down the wooden dock, his blood pulsing in his neck, his hands cold, no gun. He watched Jesse step onto another boat, a Boston Whaler just like Mathias's, open the door to the cabin below and step in.

The blood in Ray's neck pulsed harder. Jerry was a few yards behind, and Ray motioned toward the boat a dozen or so feet ahead. The white hull gleamed in the sun, reflecting the dappling waters below. Then Ray saw the name painted on the stern: *Two Feathers*, Mashpee, MA.

He boarded the boat as quietly as he could, squeaky shoes and all. Jesse opened the cabin door, shotgun by his side.

"Get off."

"You gonna steal this boat, Jesse? Just stop running for five minutes and we can help you. We know you didn't kill Mathias and that Nora was an accident."

Jesse raised the gun. Ray raised his palms.

"Don't go there. You don't have to."

"I said get off."

To Ray's surprise, the cabin door opened again. Amos "Little Drum" stepped out and put a hand on Jesse's shoulder. Two other men emerged to make sure Ray got the message. They all stood quietly, shotgun aimed at Ray, as the boat rocked gently in the harbor. Amos smiled.

"Now that we're all here, we can calm down and be reasonable. Jesse is distraught—his grandmother called, and we came to get him. He needs spiritual healing."

"Bullshit. This is a murder investigation. At the least I can bring him in for pulling a firearm on a police officer."

"But you're not an officer. You're a summer hire. A rent-a-cop. You could say an eagle that flies too close to the sun."

"No, he's not getting off on this. We've been chasing Jesse for days. He killed Nora Winnetukqet with drugs bought from Dr. Spahr. Drugs Mathias bought, gave to Jesse and Asa to get rid of Nora because she was against your casino."

"That's a lot of conclusions. If any of it's true, it's within the tribe, and we will look into it."

"This is insane. I'm taking him in." Ray grabbed Jesse's arm, and two large hands made sure he hit the deck. He could feel his insides burning. He had never felt so alone trying to do the right thing.

"Looks like it's not your day, Ray." The familiar Boston brogue chirped behind him. Ray turned violently. Busick stood next to Jerry, spinning his Oakleys in his hand, his raccoon eyes bright and twinkly.

"No. You can't let this go. The kid is in our pocket!"

Busick pursed up his lips and shook his bald, shiny head. "Not our bag. The chiefy here knows what he's doing. Spiritual healing is his jurisdiction. And I think the governor is gonna agree what happens in the tribe stays in the tribe."

"Jerry! Tell me we have leverage here. There's got to be some charge we can bring him in for. Anything. You know he was on Mathias's boat when he died and didn't go to the police. You know he ran from Spahr's office after trying to expose him for selling the drugs to Mathias. He's running from you, too. From local crimes. You have every right to charge him."

"Not your case, Ray. Dukes County got its arson charge, we cleaned up the community by getting rid a pill pusher, and like you said, the boy on the slab is just chicken of the sea. I'm sure Jesse here is in good hands. Gotta know where you fit, Ray, or you'll get burned flying too close to the wigwam, or whatever chiefy here said."

"Goddamn it." Ray pushed his way off the boat.

"Kid's got a temper. Looks like he's gonna be on disability a little bit longer." Busick winked at Jerry.

Anne emerged from the Escalade onto the dock, fanning herself. Ray was less surprised to see her this time, almost glad she was there. She would have made better backup.

"I saw the whole thing, Ray. Sweetheart, what are you gonna do?"

"I don't know, Ma. I have to get the story out. I can't believe Jesse is going to leave the island under this bullshit federal protection clause or whatever it is."

"You tell your story, and pretty soon the truth will come out and people will know you figured it out. But listen to me, you gotta let it go for now. You try to fight this and you'll never get your job back. I hate to say it."

Busick walked back and climbed into the Escalade. Anne closed the door as he drove off.

"I'm riding with you."

"I guess you are."

The three piled into the cruiser and headed back to Tisbury. Ray didn't say a word to Jerry. Didn't even look at him.

Only Anne was unfazed. "Stop at Cronig's and get me some rub-offs."

———

The rest of August was hot, boring, crowded. Ray quit SES and wandered around, looking for his reason to get up in the morning. Boston PD was mum except for the monthly disability check. Jerry called a few times, reminding Ray he did like beer and there were towns that served it.

Ray felt like a foster child on the island. Everyone smiled politely from a distance. As predicted, Andrew Cogswell's sensational arson trial might as well have tied him Christlike to the mast of the Mayflower. He played the martyr in his salty way and declared that when released from prison, he would run for town selectman and review all building codes top to bottom. Ray found this out reading the two island papers, as any outsider would, feeling like it never happened. There were a few accolades to the cooperation of Boston PD, and a picture of recently promoted Officer Jerry DeBettencourt that ran next to a story about nesting wrens on State Beach. There was no mention of Ray's name anywhere. All he had was distant and charred memories. The knife cut in his hand still hadn't healed.

One afternoon, Anne was on the porch as usual, magnifying lens in hand.

"Ray! Come over here and check these Powerball tickets and tell me if I won anything."

Ray shook his head and let the screen door slam behind him. He suddenly admired and understood his mother's stubbornness when the cards were stacked against her. He laughed.

"I'm gonna let you in on a little secret, Ma. You didn't win anything yesterday, you didn't win anything today, and you're not gonna win anything tomorrow. In fact, I've got a better idea. Why don't you give me twenty dollars and I'll light it on fire. Just as exciting. Guaranteed same outcome."

"Give an old woman a break."

Gay Head Cliffs   Photo: *Linda Zarro*

Gay Head Community Center   Photo: *Linda Zarro*

Ferry in Vineyard Haven Harbor   Photo: *Linda Zarro*

Edgartown Jail   Photo: *Linda Zarro*

BACKSTORY:
THE COURT CASES

Although *Death on Moshup's Rock* is a fictional story, it draws from the decade-long fight in federal, state, and local courts for the right of the Wampanoag tribe of Aquinnah to build a gaming facility on their tribal land. Use the links below to read more about the historically complex, highly emotional fight to claim control over the use of land, and thereby the identity, of Martha's Vineyard.

Commonwealth v. Wampanoag Tribe of Gay Head, No. 16-1137 (1st Cir. 2017)

Can be viewed online at http://media.ca1.uscourts.gov/pdf.opinions/16-1137P-01A.pdf

Commonwealth of Massachusetts v. Wampanoag Tribe of Gay Head, No. 19-1661 (1st Cir. 2021)

Can be viewed online at http://media.ca1.uscourts.gov/pdf.opinions/19-1661P-01A.pdf

ABOUT THE AUTHOR

Zoey Z. Rawlins moved to Oak Bluffs on Martha's Vineyard in 1989 with her mother and graduated from Martha's Vineyard Regional High School in 1991. While her career path strayed far from creative writing, her destination is somewhere between Raymond Chandler and Agatha Christie, where the characters are witty, and the dialogue snappy. It took just about ten years, between working for a living, having a kid, building a house, and fixing said house, to complete the book in your hands. Rawlins currently lives in Arlington, Virginia, with her husband, Ben, and their son, Thurston, and they return to the family's Oak Bluffs home every summer.

Visit the author's website at: zzrawlins.com

Connect with the author on Facebook
at: facebook.com/zoeyzrawlins

ACKNOWLEDGMENTS

It takes a small army of enormously supportive and good people over the decades to turn out a writer like myself. Let's start at the beginning. I want to thank my dad for late nights watching Philip Marlowe; my mother for keeping *The Sherlock Holmes Collection* on our shelf; my grandmother, Anne, for being, well, herself; my Martha's Vineyard Regional High School English teachers, Dan Sharkovich and Leroy Hazelton, for doing yeoman public school teacher work; my aunt, Diane Hendershot, for her constant enthusiasm and comedic relief; my beta readers Colleen McCulloch, Bill Reese, James Noll, and the Ladies Book Club of Evans, Georgia. Finally, my family and friends whose compliments I always welcomed and criticisms I dismissed.